Also by Mike Gipson:

Ocher's Dawn

Ocher's Rain

Ocher's Wind

Ocher Jones Western Series
Book Three

Mike Gipson

To   Gayle

You're always there for me.
In calm seas and high winds.

Acknowledgements

Anne Armezzani, Judy DeCarlo, Janet Schwick,

Lourdes Schaffroth, and Ann Vitale.

Ocher lives and breathes through your insight and

motivation.

Thanks again.

Anne Armezzani

Without your guidance and encouragement,
Ocher would still be trying to escape from a file cabinet
somewhere.

Kacey, Life is still out there. Go get it.

Characters –

Ocher Jones - Assassin, AKA Little Orphan, Traveler, named Shiilooshe by Ojos (Book 1)

Lewis & Amanda Livingston - Owners of the Double LL Ranch

Stacey Livingston - Daughter of Lewis & Amanda. Possible love interest

Kemen Cortez (Baja) - Mexican Bandit who befriends Ocher

Tyler Gomez – Patron of the "Best horse Ranch in the West"

Holt Sturdevant – Texas Ranger

Manny – Yaqui medicine man. Trail boss

Abel Jones – Frontiersman, friend who knows more than he should

Jorge Von Derr – Son of Ollie. (Book One)

Caufield Turner – Boatswains Mate of the *S/V Anne Belle*

And a few more.

In the dawn, the rustlers attack, and the chase begins. The herd is recovered. Ocher hopes for fair winds.

The calm before the storm is shattered by a kidnapping and a chase at sea, ending in a confrontation with enemies from the past.

Chapter One

Wind, it's good for sailors, but not much else.

Ocher crawls out of his bedroll. After putting on his sombrero, as all good cowboys do first, he pulls on his boots after shaking out any unwanted livestock. The smell of fresh coffee draws him toward the coffee pot. Manny, a Yaqui medicine man and trail boss, is standing just outside the camp site looking toward the West. "Morning, Manny. Something wrong?"

"Si, mi amigo. I have taught you many things about the desert and the medicine of the plants. Learn this also. Smell the dust in the air? Look, the Western sky is angry. The dawn colors are gone, replaced by the sand. A storm is coming. We must prepare."

Ocher has learned to trust the old Indian in all things about the desert. Manny's knowledge of the plants and animals, of what seems empty sand, seems boundless. If Manny says a storm is coming, a storm is coming.

Ocher closes his eyes, stands still and takes several breaths. His instincts tell him something's wrong, but he can't quite touch it. The horses. Opening his eyes he looks at the herd, focusing on the Pinto.

"There is something bothering you, mi amigo. What is it?" Manny asks.

"Si. There's something else. The desert has eyes. The storm's approaching from the west, but the horses are looking toward the east. There's another evil in the air."

Manny has also learned to trust Ocher's instincts. Without hesitation, "Roberto, forget the horses. Con prisa, rapidamente. Everyone to the wagons."

Ocher can hear Roberto, the Segundo, second in command, giving instructions to the other seven vaqueros, "Take cover under the wagons, mi amigos, quickly."

Ocher and Tito, the cook, rush to tie down the chuck wagon's skirts to the wheels. Every man works furiously while watching the wall of sand storm advancing toward the encampment.

Ocher and Manny watch the desert opposite the storm.

Manny stops his efforts, just for a heartbeat, "Amigo, you are right. They come!"

The banditos conduct one of the most masterful raids that Ocher has ever seen. The raiders come from the east using the storm as a distraction. The attackers overwhelm the camp, targeting the herd of horses. They try to take the wagons but the tenacity of the vaqueros and the ferocity of the storm stop the attack. They want the horses.

Four of the attackers are left afoot after colliding into each other in the blinding sand. Ocher hopes to capture at least one of them with the intent of questioning him. One of the horseless bandits runs toward the chuck wagon, trying to get on the side opposite the wind. He's gunned down by one of his own.

"Doesn't appear they intend to leave anybody behind who can reveal their location," Ocher yells at Manny over the howling wind.

Manny, whose age is anywhere between old and ancient, reaches over to get a lariat from his saddle. "I cannot just sit here. Some of mi amigos did not get under the wagons. I must go find them."

"You stay, Manny. You know the healing ways. I don't. I'll bring them in when I find them."

Ocher watches, as best he can, the direction the rustlers stampede the herd as they race out of camp. More importantly he memorizes the placement of the wounded. He's seen no sign of the Pinto or Roberto. He uncoils Manny's lariat, ties one end to a wheel and places the loop over his body. Ocher pulls his sombrero down so tight that it hurts his head, then cinches down the chin strap. He crawls out into the storm.

The sand is merciless. As Ocher tries to breathe, the sand penetrates the bandana allowing him only small gulps of air. He tries to listen but the wind is the only sound. Ocher stops. *Use your skills, trust your instincts.*

Ocher crabs along on his knees, feeling his way along. There's little difference in keeping his eyes open or closed. Only the color of the darkness, brown verses black, fills the air. Ocher rules out trying to yell out. Opening his mouth would only result in a mouth full of sand, limiting his breathing further.

Minutes seem like hours but progress is made. The desert is flat so any heap has to be a body. To Ocher's dismay he finds four of the five missing men. Two are dead; two are moved under the wagon to receive what care Manny and Tito can give.

Ocher starts to crawl back into the desert. Just as suddenly as it had begun, the storm stops. The silence is as deafening as the storm itself. Ocher stands and removes the lariat from his waist, the sand cascading from his clothes. He loosens the chin straps and with a great deal of effort removes the sombrero.

Ocher's concern over Roberto and the Pinto subside when Ocher sees the missing pair walking around the bodies of the bandits. Roberto is using his wide brim sombrero to knock the dust from his clothes. He walks toward the chuck wagon, leading a horse, the Pinto following.

The bedraggled vaquero smiles and says, "Senior Ocher, it would appear that the Pinto did not wish to go with those bad men, and he brought back a friend." Roberto accepts the canteen of water from Ocher. "I could not get to cover. I laid down and covered my head with my sombrero, and prayed. The Pinto and his senorita found me. We walked back. How can I help?"

Ocher thinks. *The owner of the herd, Senior Gomez, knows how to pick good men. Roberto has been out in the desert completely exposed to the storm and his first question is about wanting to help.* Ocher replies, "Let's see if we can help Manny and Tito with the wounded. If they don't need the help, we'll bury the others." Roberto follows Ocher toward the shelter without comment.

Manny and Tito accept the assistance of Roberto, so Ocher sets about digging graves. There's no dirt in the desert, just hardpan covered in a layer of sand. Digging in it is difficult, allowing Ocher to vent some of his anger, but not all of it. All who can, come to the grave site, gather for their last respects for their friends and six attackers.

There had been some talk about banditos when the drive left the Gomez Ranch in Sabinos, Mexico. The route chosen would be the easiest and, at the time, the safest. It ran due west to Julimes, located on the Concho River, then on to the buyer's ranch at Ures. Ten men are assigned to tend the herd with Tito in the chuck wagon. The outfit always watches for any signs of trouble but see none, until this morning.

Ocher cleans out the Pinto's nose and mouth with a wet bandana, saddles the Pinto and rides over to the chuck wagon, "Manny, I'm going to follow the herd toward the Rio Paqigochic. With all of the commotion, maybe not all the horses followed along. If there are strays, they'll stay with the water. The river is the only place for a drink. I'll be back shortly."

"Si. We will need horses for the wagons. Take care my friend. The bandito is known as Chavez."

The ride is only an hour or so, just enough time to reflect on the events of the last six months. A simple proposition: spend time with Tyler Gomez and learn about horses. The vaqueros have been eager to share their knowledge of horses and, in addition, teach Ocher Spanish. When the opportunity to make the drive west to Ures is presented, Ocher accepts the invitation. When the herd is delivered, Ocher just has to head due north and home. The timing seems perfect. Stacey will be back to the Double LL at about the same time as Ocher arrives.

The Pinto knows where the water is and which direction the herd was driven. Ocher is just along for the ride. Horse and rider arrive at the river.

There are a dozen horses of Senior Gomez grazing along both banks of the river. Ocher dismounts and talks to the horses. The small herd is none too interested in him, but eventually gather around the Pinto. Ocher takes the time to use the river water to wash out his clothes. It's so arid that the clothes are ready to wear almost immediately.

Tito is cooking when Ocher arrives. He unsaddles the Pinto and turns him loose. The other horses settle in with the Pinto and wander a short distance from the camp. The uninjured vaqueros are gathered around the coffee fire.

"Well, Manny, with those horses we can at least get out of the middle of the desert. Question is when and where do we go?"

"We will have to wait several days, mi amigo. The men will have to mend, a little anyway. There is one bullet that still needs to be removed. I will tend to it soon. It will be a long journey, regardless if we start back or go on. With the horses you recovered, there are enough to pull the wagon and for all to ride."

"I might just scout around a bit unless you think I should stay with you," Ocher says, to no one in particular.

Manny looks at Ocher, "There is nothing left for those men to come back for. Even if they did, we cannot defeat the numbers that attacked this morning. Our only enemy will be the journey. There is plenty of water no matter which way we choose and there is food in the wagon."

"The Pinto can follow the herd. That many horses can't trek across country without leaving sign. We'll find where they're holding the horses. Then I will make a plan. I'll leave in the morning".

"Those are bad and evil men. What can you do alone?" Manny asks.

Before Ocher can answer, Tito announces, "*Viveres*" food.

Around the campfire that night Ocher gleans as much information about landmarks, waterholes, and the most logical place to hold a herd of horses. The men are eager to share their knowledge about the mountains and surrounding desert. In addition, it's decided that the wounded men and wagon should go on to the buyers ranch at Ures, report the attack and loss of the horses. The ranch in Ures is three hundred miles closer than the Gomez ranch. Tito, Roberto and Ocher split the night watch, just in case. Manny attends to the wounded.

Chapter Two

The sunrise finds Ocher already at the Rio Paqigochic. The years of training as an assassin have given him confidence in his physical skills. The months of being with Manny have added to his survival skills. The Yaqui taught Ocher about the desert. It's not as desolate as it appears. If you're patient, the desert can provide water, food and the healing power of plants that grow there.

Tracking the bandits might seem impossible, but pushing a herd of around one hundred shod horses leaves a trail. The sand storm did a reasonable job of erasing some sign, but.. Ocher doesn't even have to dismount to see the horseshoe marks made on the rocks leading east by northeast, exactly as the vaqueros predicted. Ocher suspects that the bandits will eliminate any of the wounded that can't keep up, leaving additional confirmation of the trail.

"Get yourself a good drink, Pinto, then we'll get on the trail."

Ocher is following the sign toward the most likely place, a high pasture with plenty of water

located east northeast about a day's ride. The
main trails in or out will obviously be watched.
According to the vaqueros there's an old Indian
back trail. The trail can accommodate one man
on horseback. Ocher smiles thinking to himself,
A good fortress can also mean a great prison.

Although this is the fall of the year, it's still
hot. Ocher takes his time, reading the sign and
stopping to bury two men. He doesn't expect the
bandits to cover their back trail. But taking it
slow and easy seems prudent. Careless men
don't live long.

Manny and the vaqueros warn that the
entrances to the pasture will be guarded and
there may be sentries riding outside the valley.
Ocher makes a decision. He figures to make a big
swing away from the trail, coming in above the
valley, avoiding any guards or outriders.

At sunset he stops for coffee and a cold
meal. As has become his habit, he moves away
from the camp fire and settles in for the night.

The drizzling rain moves in before dawn
making sleep or rest impossible. The mist also
reduces the visibility down to about one hundred
yards. He and the Pinto can move about virtually
undetected. They start off into the Santa Maria
foot hills before sunrise. The misting rain lets up
mid-morning, Ocher stops to make coffee, and
has a piece of jerky while looking over the
terrain. If his navigation is correct he's above
the elevation of the hideout and about ten miles

west. He will move in closer and set up camp about five miles from the plateau being used by the banditos. By sunset, he'll have chosen his own hide out and start formulating a plan.

The Pinto stops dead, backs up slightly, pricks his ears and looks up toward a jumble of boulders. Ocher's instincts tell him that no attack is imminent. He dismounts and moves into a pile of rocks and tumbleweeds. The Pinto remains calm but keeps looking into the boulders. Time stops, and the air is perfectly calm. Then, a break.

Animals, birds, bees and all other wild creatures usually walk, crawl, fly or slither in pretty much a straight line. The small bird that just flew by made a radical change in flight at the spot the Pinto is watching. *Someone or something is there.* It's hot. The moisture from the morning drizzle is evaporating and making it muggy and there's no shade. Ocher decides to make a move. He leaves the Pinto and takes a wide swing around the boulder field to come in with the sun in his face, no shadow. His stalk is slow, hot and surprising.

There, in a small crease just below a large boulder, lies an Indian, no movement, no attempt to conceal or attack. Ocher starts to climb down but stops. A very colorful lizard moves away from the prone figure. Manny calls them death lizards or Gila Monsters. It's apparent that the Indian has been bitten. His left leg is discolored and swollen. Manny pointed out that the lizard bite isn't usually fatal, but will sure make a man sick. Little or nothing can be done about the bite, except to apply a salve. The recovery is pretty much up to the person bitten. The man will have to be moved, but where?

The solution is provided by the Indian, a boy. Ocher can see a faint imprint of a moccasin. Ocher follows the foot prints back to a camp. He retrieves the Pinto then checks out the hideout. He loads the boy on the pony then moves back to the hiding place. The cave is very well hidden from any casual inspection. Even then a person would have to know where the entrance is. The cave has a small tank at the back where water is collecting and even a concealed area to hide the Pinto. Ocher starts a fire, puts water on for coffee and boiling water for the Red Elm in his medicine bag.

Water Women and Ojos, Crow Indians, taught Ocher about herbs used as medicines during his summer in the Uinta Mountains of Utah. As a gift, Water Woman made Ocher a medicine bag. During the time spent with Manny, Ocher has added additional herbs to the bag.

A poultice made of the Red Elm and Witch Hazel will be applied to the wound. A tea made of Dogwood will follow when the boy can drink. The poultice ingredients are mixed up in a small decorative bowl that was lying next to the boy's traveling bag. The boy does not moan or cry out in pain when the poultice is applied to the severely swollen leg.   The recovery is up to the boy.

Although the hideout is almost perfect, Ocher spends the rest of the day setting traps, not just to warn him of anyone approaching but traps to inflict injury. Injured people will talk. Supper is coffee and a rabbit that Ocher kills with the rock sling he always carries. There's no movement or sound from the boy as Ocher reapplies the salve. The swelling seems to have stopped but the boy does have a fever. It's cool in the cave and that helps. All that can be done is being done.

Morning comes quickly, breakfast coffee made, salve applied, the Pinto watered and fed. It's time to look over the bandit's hideout. Ocher takes his Sharpe's, given to him by his friend and Texas Ranger, Holt Sturdevant, and moves out on foot in the direction where he thinks the bandits are holding the herd.

Chapter Three

The bandit's valley is about five miles long running east to west and about three miles wide. A small stream meanders through the east end of the valley. The entrance, entrances is more accurate, are at the west end. There appear to be four entrée trails, fanned out. Three of them are guarded. The fourth entrance has been made into a large corral, also guarded. A barely visible trail cuts up the east side of the valley, but no guard. The buildings consist of a hay barn, bunk house and a main house with attached veranda. Ocher counts forty-two people including half-a-dozen women but no children. He spends the entire day watching the routine of the camp before starting back to his own hideout.

The boy seems to be fighting back. The swelling is going down in the leg, and the fever is not as high as it was, but the boy remains unconscious. Ocher treats the leg and prepares his supper. After checking on the Pinto and the boy, he settles in for the night.

The cave is cool during the day and cold at night so Ocher keeps a fire going to keep the boy warm. During the morning routine, while adding wood to the fire, Ocher feels the boy watching him. He turns and, sure enough, the boy, knife in hand, is watching Ocher's every move. Ocher moves casually while making the boy the Dogwood tea. The boy hesitates but takes the cup and tries a small sip. Ocher knows exactly how the boy feels, as he spills most down the front of his chest. Ocher doesn't smile.

"I'm Ocher Jones," he says, in English and Spanish.

The boy eyes widen as he looks at Ocher's right hand. "I am," in Spanish, "Two Feathers."

Ocher continues in Spanish, "You want more tea?"

Two Feathers shakes his head, sets down the cup and says, "Very tired." Then goes back to sleep, knife in hand.

Two Feathers wakes up later in the morning while Ocher is having coffee, breakfast and tending to the Pinto. Ocher makes a cup of tea for the boy.

Ocher learns that Two Feathers watched the bandits come in with all of the horses, and he intended to steal one. His pony broke a leg while they were scouting around. He moved into the cave and was setting some game traps when he was bitten by the Gila Monster.

He then surprises Ocher. "I see the mark," pointing to the scar left by Geronimo's knife. "You are the blood brother of Geronimo?"

"Yes."

"Then you are my brother. That is good."
Two Feathers takes a sip of the tea, "There is
someone else out there watching the bandit's
camp. He is very cautious, but I see his steps.
He is not one of the bandits."

Ocher says, "I'll watch for him. I'll be gone
all day; there is food, plenty of wood and water.
You need to rest. I'm going back to watch the
bandits. I'll get you a horse in a day or so." The
boy seems amused by that thought but is too
tired to continue the conversation.

Chapter Four

Ocher takes a water bag, the Sharpes and steps through the brush hiding the cave's entrance. He stands very still listening for trouble, senses something but moves on anyway. The bees, something has disturbed the bees. Without any panic Ocher moves into concealment and starts to look for the reason the bees are in a frenzy. It doesn't take long. Someone is making coffee, and the smell is unmistakable. Ocher moves toward what may be a trap, the coffee the bait.

There he sits, the big man, dressed out in deer skins, a high caliber rifle sitting next to his leg, just like the first time they met. He has a coffee cup in his right hand and another cup, filled with coffee, sitting across from the fire. "You know I like mine with a little honey once in a while. Come on in and set." Ocher is more amused than stunned. He accepts the invitation for a cup of coffee. "Been watching you since they attacked you out in the flats. I figured you had the sand to track Chavez into these mountains. Figured maybe I could help. Don't like that bandit much. Do me good to discomfort him some. "

"Hello, Abel. You been watching me for three days?"

"No, four, I was riding parallel to your herd for a day when Chavez attacked. Don't feel too bad. I didn't see Chavez coming either. He surprised us both. How's the boy?"

Ocher's confidence is a little shaken, but he doesn't let it show. He's been followed for days and never felt Abel's presence. "The boy's recovering. You're not a surprise to him. He said there was someone out there."

Abel continues, "You been watching Chavez's camp. What you got planned?"

Ocher reveals the preliminaries of his plan.

"Boy, that's just crazy enough to work. What say we split up and spend the day watching the camp and set your plan in motion?"

Ocher stands, drains his coffee, sets down the cup. "I'll take the west rim, you take the east, meet you here at sunset. Pick up your horse and go to the cave."

Abel kicks sand onto the fire, and they head out.

The day's spent watching the routine of the camp and formulating the plan for retrieving the horses. Chavez doesn't matter, at least not right now. Ocher just wants the horses. At sunset, he's back at the small camp site waiting for Abel. They're both tired and hungry and anxious to get into the cool of the camp, at least for a little while.

Two Feathers is as surprised as Abel, when Abel leads his horse and follows Ocher into the cave.

"Two Feathers, this is Abel. He's here to help me get you a horse," Ocher introduces his friend.

Abel nods, "Two Feathers, I know your father White Elk. We have traded before. He's a man of honor as I'm sure you are."

"You are Abel Jones, also a man of honor."

Ocher appears to be the odd man out, "Abel, the Pinto's in the back, and I'll start some supper then we can finish planning."

Two Feathers remains stoic. Ocher suspects Two Feathers is as anxious to hear the plan as Ocher is to share it.

The trio have not had any time to hunt so they share some beef jerky. Two Feathers has some tea while Ocher and Abel have coffee. When the routine of the bandit's camp and the plan for retrieving the horses is discussed, all three of the men add to the plan. Two Feathers is still not able to travel the distance to the bandit's camp. He can help closer to the cave with other supplies. Well after dark, Ocher and Abel leave to begin the preparations. It's a long night and when the tired pair return to the cave at sunrise, they're done in.

To their surprise Two Feathers has coffee on when they enter. "I tried to drink your coffee. That black water is evil, even with honey." Ocher and Abel collapse as two Feathers pours the black water. "The things you asked me to find are in the next cave. I will find more later today."

Chapter Five

Ocher and Abel have some of Two Feathers' snake stew for breakfast and settle in for a quick rest. There's more to do. After a couple of hours, the two men return to their work around the bandit's camp, then at sunset they return to the cave. Two Feathers has snared and cooked a turkey along with his other chores.

During supper the plan is finalized. All three are ready for what's to come the next day and night. The details are discussed, trying to anticipate problems, and by the time they all curl up for some sleep, they're ready.

The next morning all is in readiness: the gear is packed, ammunition readied, horses saddled and fed. The extra supplies that Two Feathers has gathered are brought to the entrance to the cave. They're ready. Ocher and Two Feathers move out with the Pinto toward a position at the entrance to the valley. Abel moves to the southwest rim of the valley. They have all day to get into position. At dawn, the fun begins.

During the night Two Feathers moves toward the horses while Ocher sneaks toward the bunk house with his surprise. It's slow going. The bandits are not on alert and have grown complacent with their guard duties, but there are still guards to deal with. Inside the hay barn Ocher encounters a sleeping guard. The end is quick. No noise escapes his throat as the knife ends his life. Hopefully, no one will notice the missing guard before dawn.

The hour seems like days but finally just a hint of grey appears. The timing has to be perfect. Ocher slips to the entrance of the bunk house, sets down the basket and removes the lid. He then moves back to the hay barn just as Abel begins shooting.

Abel has taken up a sniper's position on the southeast corner of the canyon. Using Ocher's Sharpes Buffalo Gun, Abel is eliminating the guards around the entrances closest to the horses. Abel is also taking pot shots at any of the bandits that get past the basket of snakes that's blocking the entrance to the bunk house.

While all of this confusion is going on, Ocher has set the hay barn on fire and has moved toward the horses. Two Feathers opens up the coral fence on the outside of the canyon. The fire has panicked the horses into running out of the corral and out of the valley. Ocher jumps aboard a fleeing horse and leaves the valley with the panicked herd.

Abel's covering the action to discourage any of the bandits trying to follow the horses. Chavez, leader of the bandits, quickly gets control of his men and sees where the covering firing is coming from. Chavez organizes an attack on Abel's position.

However, Abel and Ocher have anticipated Chavez's response. The bandits start up and out of the valley through the rocks toward Abel's position.

"Keep coming, amigos," Abel says to the wind.

From his position, Abel directs his fire to encourage the attackers toward the dead falls, rock traps and noose snares. His shots also force the bandits into dead end pockets in the rocks. The small spaces have been seeded with snakes and Gila Monsters gathered by Two Feathers.

"Well, amigos, what you gonna do next? Take your poison, me or the critters," Abel laughs to himself.

Abel can escape at his leisure and meet with Two Feathers and Ocher out in the flats with the horses. In addition, for every injured bandit, Chavez will either have to kill them or leave them. Either way it's one less bandit to deal with. The plan works to perfection. As Abel leaves his position, he can hear the cries of confusion and agony of those who have walked into the traps. There's no pursuit.

Ocher and Two Feathers let the herd run for an hour or so, due west, before trying to slow them down, an hour of putting distance between the bandits and the herd.

Ocher rides up alongside Two Feathers. "Let's ease up a bit. They'll be too lathered up to drink when we reach the river." Two Feathers nods his agreement.

The herd slows to a manageable pace, and by the time they reach water, Abel joins them. The horses are driven on west as soon as they get water and rest a bit. The herd is well-mannered allowing the three men to easily manage them. At sunset they stop, rest for an hour or so, get water and move on into the night. Abel and Two Feathers know the trail and tell Ocher it's flat desert for the next fifty or so miles. By sunrise the herd is well away from the bandit hideout and on the banks of the Yaqui Rio. They cross the river and stop. The herd and the men need rest. The horses are glad to stop and show no signs of wandering off. Even so, one man takes a two-hour watch while the other two sleep. At noon, right after a hot meal of beans and bacon, they move the herd on toward the west.

Chapter Six

Just before sunset the men drive the herd into a box arroyo. Anticipating trouble, they build a rough corral adding several defensive positions.

Ocher has the third watch, the one just before sunrise. The sunrise with surprises. He walks over to where Abel is sleeping.

Before Ocher can speak. "What is it?" Abel says, looking up with one eye, the other eye still sleeping.

"Looks like riders coming our way."

"We figured they'd come after us."

"Not from two different directions."

Abel's up immediately. He looks toward the east and then to the west. Two Feathers joins the two men looking at the approaching dust clouds.

"Reckon we know who that is," Abel says, pointing with his chin to the east. "But who in the tar-nation could that be?" he asks, pointing his chin to the west.

There's no doubt about the trailing dust cloud. Somehow Chavez has gotten horses and is after the herd.

Two Feathers looks at the dust cloud in the east, "Those are Apaches."

Ocher and Abel look toward the east. Ocher starts, "How...?"

"See the dust? It is in a single line. You cannot count the braves. It could be many or not so many. The other dust is made by many. You can count them."

Ocher smiles at Two Feathers, "Great tactic. Your tribe?"

"We will know soon. Maybe just want the horses," Two Feathers responds.

Chavez's bandits are spread across the desert, riding hard toward the arroyo. Ocher and company have suspected that Chavez would send out scouts and discover their exact location. A scout would report the number of horses and that the herd is being wrangled by only three men. In Chavez's mind, this is an easy target.

The Apache party fans out just before intercepting the bandits. The two dust trails collide. When the dust settles, the desert floor is littered with bodies, bandit bodies. The Apaches wheel around to continue the attack. No need. In the distance there are three riders escaping the scene.

"Well blast. I didn't get to fire a shot. See that rider on the far left out yonder, Ocher?" Abel asks.

"Yep."

"That's Chavez. He won't take kindly to any of this. Powerful, revengeful. Watch your backside."

"That will have to wait. What about these folks?" Ocher points toward the arriving Apaches.

Chapter Seven

"**H**ello, father," Two Feathers greets the approaching Apache warrior leading the scouting party.

"Two Feathers," is the only response.

Two Feathers turns to Ocher and Abel, "This is my father, White Elk."

"Hola, Abel," White Elk says, looking at Abel. "It has been many moons since we have camped together."

"Yes, Chief White Elk, it has."

Ocher knows better than to speak until spoken to. He stands silently and slightly behind both Abel and Two Feathers.

"Father, this is Ocher Jones," Two Feathers begins, the remainder of the long introduction Ocher cannot understand. It's in Apache. Several times during Two Feathers' speech White Elk looks at Ocher, nods, grunts then returns his gaze to his son.

White Elk says nothing. He looks at the scene of carnage, the horses in the corral, at his son and finally dismounts. He walks directly to stand in front of Ocher.

"Ocher Jones, blood brother of Geronimo, of the Horse Clan, you have honored your clan." He stops and looks toward Two Feathers. "I am in your debt for my son's life. You will always have a place in my lodge and may travel through Apache Land without fear." White Elk turns toward the gathered warriors, "It is so."

"White Elk, I know you are a man of honor and courage. I take great pride in naming you as a friend. Two Feathers is also a man of honor and great courage. I will also call him my friend. You and he will be always be welcome in my lodge."

White Elk turns to the scouting party and issues commands in Apache. Immediately an overnight camp is set up, fires started, food prepared, wood gathered for the night and water brought in. The whole party settles in around the main camp fire.

White Elk prompts his son to tell the tale, in Spanish, of the recent adventures.

Ocher has limited experience involving the method of storytelling. Apparently Two Feathers is obligated to act out all of the individuals involved, the good and the bad. The assembled warriors laugh, gasp, and whoop as the story unfolds. Two Feathers presentation takes several hours, almost as long as the event itself. At the conclusion of the story, the warriors take turns patting Two Feathers on the back as they drift off toward their sleeping mats.

At dawn White Elk joins Ocher and Able around the camp fire. "I agree with my son. That black water is too evil to drink."

Two Feathers joins the small group and makes a face as he points toward the coffee pot, "Evil."

"Two Feathers," Ocher begins. "We could not have recovered the horses without your help. There are over one hundred horses in the corral, but only one hundred belong to Senior Gomez. That would leave about forty or so. They belong to you."

Two Feathers straightens his back and swells out his chest. "It will be counted as a great coup to return to my village with so many horses. How can I thank you?"

White Elk looks at his son and shakes his head and smiles. Finally turning toward Ocher, "We will leave tomorrow and accompany you for two days. Perhaps by then my son's pride will soften."

The day is filled with treating the wounds of the warriors and burying the dead bandits. The spoils of the battle were also gathered: guns, knives and to Ocher's horror, scalps. The water bags are filled and deer meat smoked as jerky.

That evening Two Feathers and White Elk come and sit with Ocher and Abel at the camp fire. Two Feathers, looking very serious, says,

"Ocher Jones, you have given me much to celebrate since our meeting, most of all a friendship. I have nothing to offer you, but these small things." He hands Ocher a medallion made of silver, turquoise, jasper and gold in the shape of a sunflower. There is also a small, elaborately-colored beaded pouch.

Ocher's speechless. He understands the importance of gift giving. The beaded pouch is from Two Feathers but the Concho, although presented by Two Feathers, is from White Elk. Ocher accepts the gifts with great reverence and puts the Concho around his neck. "Thank you, my friend."

The Apaches stay with the herd for two more days, then the bandit's horses are cut out and with Two Feathers in the lead, sitting very proudly on his new horse, the band moves off to the northwest back to the Arizona Territory. Abel and Ocher set off to the west and head for Ranch Ures. If all goes well, in a week they'll meet up with Manny and the trail crew.

Chapter Eight

Abel, leading the trail herd, rides up to the vaquero stationed in front of the oncoming herd.

Manny's sitting in the saddle with his hands folded over the saddle horn, "Buenos Diaz, Senior Abel." Manny leans to his left and looks over Abel's shoulder at the herd of horses. "We see the dust, but do not think it possible that it could be the horses. How is this possible? Two men?"

"Three. Ocher and I had some help."

Manny looks again past Abel and sees the Concho hanging around Ocher's neck, "An Apache?"

"Yep. It's quite a story. I'll be glad to tell it after something other than trail grub."

"Si, mi amigo. I will go and send some more men to help," Manny says, turning his horse.

"No need. Here comes some help."

About a dozen Vaqueros from the ranch ride to the herd. They fan out and drive the herd across the river onto an area with knee high grass. The horses move to the meadow and settle in.

Ocher and Abel ride with Manny to the chuck wagon and are enthusiastically greeted by Tito and Roberto. Tito seems very surprised. "Senior Abel, it has been a very long time." Abel just nods, too tired to get real excited.

Ocher asks, "The men?"

Manny smiles, "All are well and ready to return home, maybe a day or so more. We were waiting for you to return. All of mi amigos are ready to ride against the bandits and bring back the horses. They will be disappointed. You must tell the tale."

The Patron of Ranch Ures provides a steer to be roasted and all that goes with it. Ocher and Abel take full advantage. Manny and the rest of the vaqueros are anxious to hear the story of the recovery of the horses. It doesn't take much prompting to get Abel to reenact the whole adventure.

By the conclusion of the story, they are heroes of much more than just recovering the horses. Abel can tell a tale. The gathering around the camp fire is most impressed with the part of the story when White Elk is mentioned. The confrontation with Chavez is impressive but the Apaches are the center of attention. The tale goes on 'til the wee hours of the morning and grows more elaborate with every telling.

Ocher cashes in long before the rest of the gathering and sleeps well past sunrise, stirring only when Tito brings coffee. The next two days are taken at a leisurely pace, inspecting and selling the herd, outfitting the chuck wagon for the return trip and letting the wounded heal. During that time Abel decides to make the return trip with Manny to Sabinos.

Ocher makes other plans, "Manny, I will be returning to Pine Creek. There's much to do before spring and well, there is someone."

"Si, Senior Ocher, I understand. Being a cowboy is a lonely life. Much better to have someone and someplace to have as a home." Manny knows exactly how Ocher feels.

"I'll head north to El Paso. I shouldn't have any Apache trouble and I'll stay well west of Chavez. As long as the rains hold off, I should make the trip in ten days or so. I'll leave when you start east."

The morning dawns bold and glorious. It's a clear sky, a good omen. The business of leaving gets under way. All of the Vaqueros from the Gomez ranch can ride and are anxious to start the long journey home. The Adiós are exchanged with a Via Con Dios thrown in. Ocher's ready to start back to Pine Creek and start making High Range a home. The Pinto is rested and as ready as Ocher to start out.

At the nooning of the first day, Ocher watches the dust trail of the herd diminish and disappear in the east. Ocher drinks the last of his coffee, kicks dirt over the fire and walks over to the Pinto. "You ready, horse? You didn't think I'd let Chavez trail us back home did you?"

The Pinto listens intently, enjoying the rub along his muzzle.

Ocher looks back to the last position of the herd. "Chavez, you're not stupid enough to take on the trail herd, not alone anyway. You already know what the Apaches can do. So It's gotta be me. The lone rider."

The Pinto stamps his foot, signaling his impatience.

"All right, horse, let's get to it." Ocher steps into the saddle riding due north.

For the remainder of the first day Ocher rides pretty much a straight line taking a bearing on a cut in the line of low hills. Making a show of setting up an evening camp, he roasts a prairie chicken, *Grouse*, gathers wood and sets out his bedroll. He isn't in the bedroll long before the camp is abandoned. The moon provides enough light for Ocher to see the reference point in the hills north.

When the moon disappears in the west, Ocher and the Pinto are ten miles from the original camp. Ocher dismounts, rubs down the Pinto with the saddle blanket and turns him loose knowing that his traveling companion will alert him if another rider comes along. Taking his bedroll Ocher finds a niche in the small pile of rocks and settles in for the remainder of the night.

At dawn, Ocher is up and spends over an hour with his spy glass checking his back trail. Satisfied that he has time for coffee and some bacon on skillet bread, he cooks. "Might be the last decent meal I get for a while," he addresses the Pinto.

Ocher takes a fair amount of time to hide the overnight camp knowing any trail wise hand will eventually find it. His efforts are made to slow down any pursuer.

Ocher no longer travels in a straight line. He doubles back through soft sand, stays below the ridge line of even the lowest of hills. By the end of the day Ocher and the Pinto are not far from the original night camp. Ocher has ridden in a very wide circle. Anyone trailing him will have to parallel the trail and Ocher can now cross his own sign and see if there are now two sets of tracks, his and the follower. The evidence is there, a single rider on a tired horse. The horse is dragging his feet making an elongated print. A fresh horse will make a clean print. Ocher makes an assumption: if the horse is tired so is the rider. "Horse, let's not let them rest long."

Ocher climbs up on a jumble of boulders. Lying on his stomach he studies the direction of the trail. It's not much, just a barely visible flare. *Must want a hot meal. I wouldn't take a chance of starting even a small fire. Tired men make mistakes.*

Ocher ponders whether he should reveal his presence or keep the pursuer on the move. He decides on the tired man approach. Ocher steps into the saddle and moves to within one thousand yards of the man's camp, steps down and unsheathes his Sharpes. Taking careful aim he fires two shots into the area of the firelight. There's no return fire. Ocher steps into the saddle and rides away. "He may be tired but still plenty dangerous. Besides this is his desert and not my jungle," Ocher says to the Pinto.

Ocher gives the Pinto his head and the pair move off to the west for several hours of no moon. They rest for a few hours at dawn and then head north toward the mountains and El Paso.

Ocher is thinking, *Where would I be if I was Chavez? The mountains. Take to the high point.*

Ocher rides into a low arroyo, dismounts and lets the Pinto loose. As the Pinto walks out of the dry wash, Ocher sees a flash of light. The bullet grazes the Pinto's neck just above the pommel. The horses reaction is one of annoyance, like being stung by a bee.

Ocher waits, listens and watches the Pinto for any sign that the shooter's coming to finish the job. Nothing happens. "Well, we can't stay here. Chavez knows exactly where we are. Waiting to ride out in the full moon light won't work either." Ocher unsaddles the Pinto, treats the horse's wound then moves his gear up the lip of the arroyo, above what appears to be the flood line. Ocher takes the water bag, the Sharpes and moves down the arroyo toward the direction the shot came from. Surely, the shooter has moved from the original position. "I'll be back in a couple days, horse."

Ocher takes a couple of guesses, *the shooter is Chavez and he'll probably move to his right toward the arroyo*. Ocher has seen Chavez only once during the confrontation with the Apaches. He was shooting with his right hand. Most people given a choice to turn right or left will normally turn in the direction of their dominant hand. *Good a guess as any.* Ocher walks to end of the arroyo and starts out, very slowly, crawling toward a low out crop of boulders. He makes the cover without incident and picks and moves from cover to cover for several hours. No shooting and no surprises. He decides that the best advantage is to approach the shooter from behind.

Moving slowly all night, Ocher is well above the shooter's original position by dawn. He finds the right vantage point and settles in to watch the valley for any sign of movement. It's going to be a long day, but he has some jerky, plenty of water and patience.

There, just a shadow of movement, bait. He doesn't know where Ocher is and wants a clue. Ocher doesn't take the bait, but now knows where to watch. The shooter is good, has patience and undoubtedly knows this terrain better than Ocher, but Ocher knows men. He has guessed correctly. The shooter is moving to his right at least for now. The deadly game continues. From his perch, Ocher can see the Pinto well off in the distance, grazing not far from the arroyo.

The day wears on, with just fleeting glimpses of Chavez as he moves. Now the bandit is trying to move to higher ground to do what Ocher's doing. It's time to move. Time to set a trap before a trap is set for him.

Day two begins with a rain shower. No need to hunt up water. Ocher fills his water bag from a small runoff waterfall after drinking his fill. The rain is the final piece to his puzzle. For the remainder of the day, Ocher continues the ruse. Let Chavez think he's chasing when in fact he's being led.

Day three, Ocher starts making calculated mistakes. Mistakes Chavez will find and follow.

On the fourth day, the change in the weather. Exactly what Ocher's been waiting for. Time to spring the trap. After three full days, the shooter will assume Ocher is continuing to make mistakes. Ocher waits and watches the bait. It's taken, not the man, just a shadow. Ocher moves just enough to show movement and entice the man forward. Ocher's protected as he moves away from the trailing man and can't be seen. The pursuer will have to work a little at the game.

All day Ocher leads the man, just a tiny bit of encouragement. The weather will break soon and rain will pummel the desert. The timing of the trap will have to be perfect.

Ocher enters the high walled arroyo as sunset begins, leaving just a hint of a broken branch at the entrance. The shooter will have Ocher cornered in this dead end canyon of limestone and he'll just wait for Ocher to come out. The trap, however, is not inside the arroyo, but outside. There's only one place to hide to cover Ocher's arroyo, a small dead end shallow cave, a death trap. The shooter thinks there's only one way in and out of the arroyo that Ocher has entered. He's wrong.

Ocher climbs up and out of the canyon though a tiny hole then moves to a well camouflaged hiding place overlooking the cave. Ocher can see Chavez now waiting and watching.

The rain comes down in gallon buckets. Visibility is reduced to next to nothing and the shooter thinks that the water will force Ocher out of the arroyo. Then it happens: a debris dam from a previous storm that's been holding back the water in Ocher's arroyo breaks. The water rushes out of the canyon. The wave, carrying boulders, pieces of the debris dam, and sand is at least ten feet high and moving faster than the shooter can move. The bandit tries to escape, just as a bolt of lightning lights the sky. Chavez sees Ocher standing atop the arroyo entrance. Then as quickly as the lighting lit the sky, the wave and all of the debris hits Chavez. It's over in an instant. He's gone.

The rain and wind doesn't stop. The desert is overwhelmed, filling up every arroyo, ravine and low spot. Ocher thinks of the Pinto, but knows he's smart enough to find shelter. He was living in the wild when Ocher came along. The rain continues all night, but Ocher's dry and warm in the ambush shelter he had built anticipating the rain.

Ocher has the last of his jerky. There are additional supplies with his kit. Water's not a problem, it's everywhere. He takes a deep breath and starts out of the mountains toward the Pinto. The temperature isn't too bad, and, with nothing to eat, Ocher doesn't stop. He walks all day. At sunset Ocher arrives back at the wash out where this all began. The Pinto is gone.

Reading the sign, the Pinto was taken by two riders on unshod ponies. The Pinto didn't go willingly. Ocher's outfit is cast about. He can see his coffee pot and cup under a creosote bush. With luck the coffee itself is still in the beat up pot. From the sign it must have been quite a struggle. *Grab a tiger by the tail.* The saddle with attached gear is gone, not by the riders but by the storm. *It's a long walk to El Paso. Best get started.*

Chapter Nine

After six days on foot in the desert, the small spring is pure pleasure. The water's sweet and cold. The area around the spring will fulfill all his needs for a good campsite for the night.

He chooses a spot well away from the spring in the lee side of a weathered jumble of rocks. There's enough of an overhang to keep the rain off if it comes in again. He's high enough from the arroyo bottom in case of a flash flood.

During his one hundred mile walk he has had to hold up twice because of flash floods. At least there's plenty of water. Food is a problem. For the most part Ocher had been surviving on snake. *It sure don't taste like any chicken.* Bringing down small game with the Sharpes just leaves a mess. The other edible critters don't fancy the heat of the day, making his rock sling almost useless.

After getting a fire started and gathering a pile of fuel, he decides to take care of his feet.

Ocher moves down stream of the spring where a small pool has formed. After removing his boots and dumping out the sand, he lowers his feet into the pool of crystal clear water. The cold water actually makes his feet hurt, but just in passing. The overall sensation is pure pleasure.

When you make a mistake in the desert you pay for it. Ocher has made the mistake of getting complacent. Sitting there with his feet in the water, the Sharpes out of reach and forgetting, just for an instant, where he is. Just how high a price will he pay?

He's being watched. The entirety of his error comes into focus when the hair on his neck stands up. He's vulnerable and deciding on what to do next when the sound comes. In his short life of twenty-one years, he's traveled more than most. But nothing prepares him for the sound coming from the rocks fifty feet in front of him.

Once in San Francisco he watched a parade with a brass band. A big horn was being played. The sound was low and melodious. The sound from the desert is similar but certainly not melodious. Ocher stands slowly and studies the area of the sound.

He's stunned by the sound but that is nothing compared to seeing what steps out from behind the boulder. To add to his disbelief, a similar sound comes from behind him. He turns and sure enough, they have him surrounded.

Growing up in an assassin's training camp the only exposure to the outside world were the stories the others brought back from an assignment. One such story involved these creatures. A tong member had traveled to Egypt and brought back a tale of huge animals that carried men across the desert.

Ocher is surrounded by three camels. *Tall buffalos. How did Geronimo know?* The one in front, the source of the original sound, is a big male. The two behind him appear to be a female and baby. The animals watch as Ocher picks up his boots and walks toward his campsite.

The big male, with the pomposity of a king, sniffs the air then in a comical gait moves off toward the campfire. The other two beasts follow his lead.

Ocher makes two decisions. First, trust the camels same as he would the Pinto. They will alert to any danger. Second, go about his business and see what they'll do.

After putting coffee on to boil, Ocher skins out a snake. All of the camp activity's being closely watched by the camels and they're listening as Ocher talks softly to them. With the snake on a skewer roasting over the fire and with a cup of coffee in hand, Ocher leans up against a rock to observe the camels.

The smallest one, the baby, wanders off into the desert to eat the prickly pear blooms. Mama camel follows along to keep the little one out of trouble. The male moves toward the campsite inch by inch, seemingly assured by Ocher's talking. When supper's ready, Ocher pushes off the rock and moves slowly toward the fire, speaking softly the entire time. The distance between Ocher and the male camel closes. The big beast is not intimidated. He stands his ground, sniffs the air and inches closer to Ocher.

The campfire is between Ocher and the camel, giving Ocher at least some level of security. But the closer the big male gets, the bigger Ocher realizes he is. The camel is nine foot at the shoulder and fifteen feet or taller when standing with his head in the air. Ocher sets his coffee aside and starts to peel meat off the skewer. The camel moves cautiously around the fire, sniffs the coffee and with all of the grace of a falling tree, leans down and sticks his tongue into the cup for a taste. His head shoots up and, with a rumble deep in his throat, he spits out the coffee.

He cocks his head to one side looking at Ocher with one eye, with an expression that seems to say, *It doesn't taste as good as it smells.* But he doesn't move away.

Ocher looks up at the big guy. "Seems to me you been around human folks before. Then again as big as you are, you can't be afraid of much." He extends his hand, fingers tucked in for the camel to smell. Instead of sniffing the hand, the camel rubs his muzzle against Ocher's hand wanting to be scratched.

Ocher abides by the request and scratches the big guy's muzzle up as far as he can reach. Not to be left out, the female walks into the camp and presents herself for the same treatment. The baby watches from a ways off still eating the prickly pear blossoms.

The rubdown continues until the sun goes behind the mountains to the west and Ocher explains, "I need to gather a bit more fuel for the fire before it gets too dark."

With Ocher in the lead and the male close behind, followed by the female with the baby in tow, they gather wood. A scene as natural as can be, a man and three camels in the desert, in Mexico.

Bedding down for the night is the same as it was on the walk. Pick your spot, clean out the rocks and settle in for the night. The only real difference is the conversation. Camels don't tell any good tales. The newly formed caravan snuggle down for the night around the campfire with Ocher doing all of the story telling.

The morning routine brings no new surprises. Man and camels go into the desert to take care of business. The camels eat breakfast before returning to the campsite to watch Ocher have coffee and leftover snake. Luckily the big male's taste for coffee has been satisfied.

Then the big surprise. Just as Ocher is getting ready to continue walking toward El Paso the big male walks right up to him and kneels down on his forelegs. Riding is certainly better than walking the remaining hundred miles.

Ocher climbs aboard and grabs a handful of neck hair. When the big guy stands up Ocher is nine feet above the desert floor. He settles in as best he can and nudges the camel forward with a light touch of his heels.

The first hundred yards are a fight for stability. The camel's gait is a whole lot different from the Pinto's. It takes about fifteen minutes, but, after Ocher catches onto the rhythm, the ride smooths out.

With Ocher's stride he was covering approximately 25 miles per day in a straight line. The camel's pace will cover twice that distance.

At noon the male camel brings the caravan to a small water tank and halts. He kneels down and Ocher disembarks with the saddlebag, holding the coffee and coffee pot. It takes him a couple of steps to get his legs under him. Riding a camel is certainly a different motion than a horse. His muscles are sore from the unaccustomed motion.

He waits for the camels to drink from the tank before filling the coffee pot and his water bag but his guests are out in the desert rolling around in the sand. He gathers some dry wood for a fire, dips out some water and puts the coffee on to boil. There's one piece of dried snake left for the meal.

After finishing their bath, the camels each take more water, first the baby, then the female and then the male. Next on the agenda is a nap.

The family eases into the shade of a rock formation and are asleep in minute. Ocher had not considered stopping, but agrees with the respite. Rest during the heat of the day then move on. Besides they have already covered twice the distance in half a day as Ocher would have covered in a full day.

He moves back into the shade of an overhanging rock and considers the camels. *How they got here should be an interesting story. Maybe Holt or Bug will know. El Paso is in for a big surprise when this group rides in.*

Every creature within hailing distance knows it's time to depart. The announcement is made by the male as he arises. The bellow echoes from the foothills back into the camp. After one more quick drink for all, Ocher mounts up and the group continues northeast toward Texas.

The progress of the camels is amazing. Uphill, downhill or on the flat desert the pace remains constant, mile after mile without Ocher taking one step.

About an hour before sunset the male, 'Hump', as Ocher has named him, deviates from the trail they've been following all day. Hump leads the family off into a maze of arroyos and small foothills. They arrive in a lush, green, open valley with a stream running down the middle. Remnants of a homestead are visible in the cluster of trees about half way down the mile long valley.

Hump ambles over to what's left of a one room adobe building, stops, and kneels down for Ocher to dismount. The day's travel has concluded and a better campsite couldn't have been chosen. There's water, shelter, fuel for a fire and Ocher can hear the cackling of a desert hen.

No snake tonight. His traveling companions have crossed the stream and make camp in a cluster of brush and tall grass.

The trip to El Paso takes just over a week with Ocher providing the general direction. Hump is the real guide. He knows the location of the water holes and the best campsites. The female has become 'Calliope'. Her voice has a wide range and is far more melodious than Hump's. The baby is now 'Blossom'. She enjoys any type of desert flower bloom and with the trip being made in the rainy season, the desert is alive with blooming plants.

Ocher stops the group on a low mesa overlooking the Rio Grande. El Paso is just across the river. *I wonder what type of reception this will get from the range-hardened, weather-beaten, and rawhide cowboys of Texas.* He doesn't really care. He just ponders on it before moving Hump down into town. The camels have provided not only the transportation across the desert but have been good company. It would have been a mighty long and lonely walk without them.

Now if he can just figure out how to get them to hunt meat.

The group halts in the middle of the river for a drink and then proceeds. The first building they come to is a blacksmith shop and livery stable. Hump stops and kneels and Ocher steps down with the same motion and aplomb as he would from the Pinto. "Howdy."

The blacksmith looks, without a bit of surprise in his voice or eyes. "I don't have any shoes that'll fit any of that bunch." He smiles as he walks out toward Ocher. "Been awhile since I seen any of Beale's Camels. I'd like to hear the story sometime how you came on 'em."

Ocher's more than surprised at the blacksmith's comment but quickly realizes they had to come from somewhere. "You got a place we can hold up for the night?"

"Why sure. In fact 'bout half a mile up behind the livery is the corral the General himself used to use. There's a lean-to still standing and a fresh water spring. Son, you know them camels are a curiosity so you'll have visitors as soon as the word gets out."

"Thanks. Maybe I should charge folks to look so I can pay you."

"No need to pay me. I used to enjoy watching them critters."

Ocher starts around the stable with Hump, Calliope and Blossom in tow. Hump seems to recognize the corral and steps up the pace arriving at the lean-to well before Ocher. Hump apparently approves of the place and, with a voice that can be heard to the other end of El Paso, lets the whole town know.

Ocher intends to leave at first light for Pine Springs but needs supplies for the trip. The camels are settling in, so he walks into town for the supplies and supper. A couple of curious folks from town have walked up to see the camels, most of them keeping their distance.

Ocher's tired and hungry. He decides to walk into town, grab a meal and a treat for the camels. At the edge of town a short, brown skinned man walks up to Ocher, "*Hugasan ang damit*, wash clothes?" The question is in Filipino.

Ocher turns and replies, "*Walang*," 'no,' in Filipino. Ocher realizes his mistake but can do nothing about it now. He continues on into town.

After a meal of beef stew, biscuits and apple pie, Ocher heads back toward the corral with his tote of new supplies and a bag full of apples for his new friends.

Three old friends are milling about at the corral harassing the camels. The boys haven't changed much since the encounter on the porch the day he met Holt.

"Afternoon, boys," Ocher says, as he walks up to the corral and takes out an apple for Blossom.

"We been hoping to meet you again. Friends of yours?" The older of the trio asks.

"Yep."

"Ugliest things I ever did see," he says, sneering at Ocher then at Blossom.

"Must not have any mirrors around here," Ocher replies.

Blossom, with the ease she has demonstrated when nibbling a cactus flower, takes a bite of the ruffian's sombrero and of course, a great deal of scalp. Hair, scalp, and a lot of blood hit the ground accompanied by a scream of pain.

The man reaches up with his left hand to replace the patch of skin previously removed and reaches for his gun with his right hand.

"I wouldn't do that," comes a familiar voice. Holt and the Pinto are standing just behind Ocher, the .44 and Ranger Badge in full view.

"Best get on over to the Doc before any more damage is done. Now git."

The Pinto has moved to Ocher and, after a nose snuggle, turns his attention to Blossom. *A new Friend?*

"That Pinto showed up this morning. Figured you might need some assistance. We were headed out when I heard about some cow hand riding in on a camel. Who else could it be?" he states.

Ocher introduces Hump, Calliope and Blossom.

"I also heard that you might have had some trouble with a very bad hombre, Chavez."

"We met."

"Might want to watch your back with that one. He don't forget. He's a bad one."

"Not anymore," is all Ocher says.

Chapter Ten

"Good morning, Maggie," Stacey says as she enters the kitchen and picks up a coffee mug. The aroma of bacon, eggs and fresh baked goods always makes her think of home. She smiles back at the remaining kitchen staffers, as is her morning ritual.

Maggie turns and gives Stacey *the look.*

"Ok, Ok," Stacey responds, sets down the mug then picks up a china cup and saucer. After pouring herself a cup of coffee, she daintily takes a sip, making sure to raise her pinky. She has grown fond of the plump black kitchen boss. Just once she wants to pour her coffee into the saucer and slurp it but doesn't want to be on the end of *the real look.*

"Miss Stacey, we're sure gonna miss you 'round here. It's hard to believe your year is almost up. Three weeks and then you head home," Maggie offers Stacey a serving dish with doughnuts. "Your mom's recipe."

Stacey takes one of the fresh bear claw doughnuts, dunks it in the coffee and smiles at Maggie, making sure she sees the raised pinky.

"Girl, I should have never let you in my kitchen, but I'm sure glad I did. Mrs. Barrington weren't too pleased 'bout you being out here neither. She kinda hushed up after I served up some of the cooking your mom learned you. Your cowboys sure eat good."

Stacey steps in close to the rotund black cook, "I won't miss the Barrington Young Ladies Finishing School but I sure will miss you, Maggie. The other girls don't know what they're missing sleeping 'til almost noon with primping and prissing around 'til lessons and lunch. Three weeks," she whispers.

"You picked out a young man to take you to the graduation dance?"

"Yes, but he's in Mexico on a trail drive. As far as men go, there hasn't been one around here yet."

Maggie laughs, "Won't argue that point with you but that's all there is. I don't think your Ocher's gonna make it here as much as I'm sure he'd like to. At least that's the impression I get from the letters you read to me. He sounds like something. That Holt fella that writes you sounds like something, too."

Stacey breaks into a big smile, "They are a pair to draw to."

"Young ladies do not play the kind of cards where you draw to a pair," Mrs. Barrington chimes in as she enters the kitchen. The six-foot, straight-backed queen of the school accepts the offer of a cup and saucer from one of the kitchen staff. She remains motionless, holding the service until the coffee is poured, then one spoonful of sugar and a dollop of cream are added. Only then does she turn to face Stacey.

"Really, and how would you know that?" Stacey inquires.

"Irrelevant, Miss Livingston. Proper ladies do not mingle with the kitchen staff as you have been told on more than one occasion. Why are you here?"

Stacey smiles and offers the serving dish of doughnuts to Mrs. Barrington.

"Oh yes. At least you are using a cup and saucer. Please finish here and go somewhere else and quit associating yourself with the help." She turns to leave but reaches back for a few more doughnuts before disassociating herself from the staff.

"I wouldn't underestimate her, Miss Stacey," Maggie says.

"No. I suspect there's more to her than what she lets on," Stacey replies, "A lot more."

Stacey considers sitting down on the edge of the preparation table but knows the rebuke that would follow from Maggie. "May I please have two eggs, bacon and two slices of that homemade bread with some peach preserves? I'll be in the dining room."

Maggie smiles, "As long as you don't use the bread to sop up the egg yolk when you finish."

"Yes, Maggie."

"Good morning, Dorothy Leigh," Stacey says, as she wipes her bread around the plate. "You're up early. Special occasion?"

"I have gentlemen callers today and I must look my best."

"Dorothy, we all have gentlemen callers almost every day."

"Only my friends call me Dorothy. Dorothy Leigh if you please."

"I notice that the other girls don't call you Dorothy. Why is that?"

"You are correct. I do not consider you or the others here as friends or, to be frank, equals," she says, as she rings the silver servant's bell.

Fredrick, the only man from the kitchen staff, arrives. "Yes?"

"I'll have a poached egg, with a sliced and peeled apple."

"Would you care for a fresh doughnut?"

"Heavens no. Fried dough, how ghastly."

"Fredrick, I'd like one if you don't mind," Stacey says.

"Miss Stacey, it would be my pleasure," he says, smiling at Stacey and ignoring Dorothy Leigh.

"Gentlemen callers. My guess is one caller, Charles Mercer," Stacey challenges.

"The only one that counts, yes, Charles Mercer."

"You two are meant for each other. Soft hands, soft bodies, educated but not too bright. A match made in heaven."

"I, we, will want for nothing. Travel, fine clothes and servants to attend to everything. You're just jealous. You have to be."

"Dorothy, I hope you get exactly what is coming to you. Jealous isn't the word I'd use. Maybe sympathy is more correct. You can't fathom my world."

Fredrick enters carrying two plates. He sets down Dorothy Leigh's. On the plate is a poached egg, sliced and peeled apple and a doughnut.

She looks at Fredrick and, in a huff, stands and walks out.

"Must've slid off your plate onto hers. Ghastly of me," he smiles.

"Ghastly," Stacey repeats, reaching for the fried dough.

After finishing her bear claw, she stands, reaches for the silver bell, as she always does, and hides it in the silver service chest. A game she taunts the other girls with. Now they will have to go into the unfamiliar world of the kitchen or actually make an effort to find the bell. It doesn't really matter. The majority of the attendees will not be up for breakfast anyway.

Passing Fredrick on her way out of the dining room, "Silver service chest," she whispers.

He acknowledges with a nod.

Chapter Eleven

High tea. Stacey smiles to herself. *I can just imagine having the hands come in from the range, dress up, sit around sipping tea in the middle of the day. New York people sure have a sense of humor if they think this is productive. At least during High Tea, you can eat the food with your fingers and not have to consider the appropriate utensil.*

"Mr. Thergood Hightower," Franklin announces. A middle-aged, average-height, average this and that gentleman enters the sitting room.

"Ah, Miss Stacey, just the person I wish to speak with," he says, ignoring the other ladies in attendance.

Stacey acknowledges Terry, as she has named him in her mind, with a nod. *He's going to ask me to the dance,* she thinks to herself. *He's probably the most harmless. Why not?*

"Would you join me for a walk in the garden?" he asks.

"Certainly, Mr. Hightower," she responds. In her mind she's thinking, *Anything to get out of this stifling room overpowered with whatever perfume the other girls have doused themselves with. The men smell no better. How I miss the aroma of saddle soap.*

Terry offers his arm and she accepts.

It isn't really a garden, just a few flowers and a tree or two ringed by a brick wall and wrought iron fence. Doesn't smell much like a garden either, in the midst of New York City.

They sit at one of the stone benches, "Mind if I smoke a cigar?" Terry asks.

"Fine," she responds.

"These afternoon teas are quite relaxing. I enjoy them very much. Especially with you," he says, lighting his cigar. "The pressure of managing our family's money is oppressive. You wouldn't understand. I sometimes wish I could do what your family does, buy cows, let them have others cows and then sell them. That's a simple life with no stress. Just sit and watch them grow," he offers.

"Yes, that would be simple," Stacey replies. "What did you want to see me about?" she questions, wanting to end the encounter.

"Yes, well, would you accompany me to the dance?"

"Which dance would that be?"

"Please, I don't have time for this. Your graduation dance, of course."

"Fine, I will attend the dance with you. The dance only, nothing else, understand?"

"Yes, I understand. You have some cowboy somewhere. I have business to attend to. Let me escort you back to the parlor."

Stacey is somewhat confused. *Terry usually overstays his visits but not today. He really must have business to attend to. He does look a little unnerved. His usual impeccable shirts and jacket are a bit tattered and mussed*, she observes as they stroll back to the house.

Franklin is standing just outside the parlor with a big smile on his face. "Mail has arrived."

Trying to stay calm and ladylike she asks, "Did I receive anything?" The smile on Franklin's face is a giveaway.

"Let me see. Your mother, Holt and someone named Ocher. There are two from him," he hands the correspondence to Stacey and steps out of the way to avoid being knocked down as she gracefully gallops to her room to read.

"I will send up some lemonade," he says.

The next morning Maggie is waiting impatiently for Stacey to arrive in the kitchen, so she can hear about the exploits of Ocher the cowboy.

"Good morning, Maggie. May I have some coffee, please?"

Maggie hands her a mug, "You can't tell good stories over china, now give, what's he been up to?"

"You sure you want to hear 'bout this? It's so boring. Besides you seem more interested in him than me."

"Girl, excuse me, Miss Livingston. If you don't start sharing, you will be banned from this here kitchen," Maggie says with a smile.

"Ok. Not much to share. He chased some horse thieves, saved an Apache Chief's son, lost his horse to some different Apaches, walked across the desert until he met up with some camels, rode one of them into El Paso and met up with Holt. See? Nothing much."

From behind Stacey, "Maggie, you are quite correct. You cannot appreciate that kind of story over a cup of coffee. Please pour me a mug. Continue, Miss Livingston," Mrs. Barrington states, sitting down at the table.

The complete kitchen staff has stopped and is listening as Stacey recounts the tale conveyed in Ocher's and Holt's letters.

Chapter Twelve

"You all look gorgeous. Just remember you are all ladies. Do not let the events of this evening sway you. This past year you have been taught the proper etiquette expected of sophisticated young ladies. Enjoy the evening. Your suitors will be arriving and will be announced shortly," Mrs. Barrington says.

"Mr. Hightower for Miss Livingston," Franklin announces.

Stacey is amused. Terry on time, that's unusual.

Thergood approaches Stacey, bows slightly and offers his arm.

She notes that Terry is perspiring and acting nervous. "Are you all right?"

"Fine, fine. We should go. I have a bit of business to handle on the way. It will detain us for just a moment. We'll be on time, not to worry," he responds.

His agitation is so obvious, he almost steps into the carriage ahead of Stacey but stops himself. "We must go."

"Where are we going for this business, Terry?" Stacey asks.

"Not to worry. Just relax. It will be over soon."

"What will be over?"

"Just business. That's all, just business."

They arrive at the docks alongside a cargo ship making preparations for getting underway. The men on the ship are taking in the ropes tying the ship to the wharf. There are men aloft in the sails. The whole scene is unsettling.

Terry steps out of the coach, turns to Stacey, "I'm sorry, really but my family needs the money," as he starts to walk away.

From the interior of the carriage Stacey can see Terry walking away but before she can ask what he meant, Terry is attacked by a man with a wooden club and knocked unconscious.

A small dark skinned man steps to the carriage door, "Miss Livingston, it would be wise if you came along quietly, so you're not treated the same as your companion," he offers his hand to Stacey.

Stacey casually reaches into her clutch purse, draws her Derringer and fires both barrels at the man. She's stunned by how quickly the man reacts. Not a scratch. She is too slow to move as the man enters the carriage and, with one motion, slaps Stacey alongside the head and renders her unconscious.

She awakens, feeling the fore and aft pitching of the ship. Still dressed in her gown, she stands and stumbles out of her cabin and onto the deck. She's used to the endless prairie with sand and tumble weeds but not horizon to horizon water.

"Good Morning, Miss, I am Captain Russell. You'll be with us for a while. You can make it easy on yourself and have the run of the ship or you can be placed under lock and key in your cabin."

"What do you want with me?"

"You and your companion are just cargo to me. I've been paid to transport you. That's all I know and care about. I made the deal with Abad. Surly little man. Don't expect he'll tell you much. Neither will the other one. Don't know his name. They speak Filipino for the most part. I get the feeling you're just the bait for someone else. Don't put much stock in that. It's just a feeling."

Stacey looks around the deck, "Where is Terry? Is he all right?"

"Your companion ain't much for sailing. He came on deck, went to the rail and went directly back to his rack."

"Where are we going?"

"Can't say. That was in my agreement. Like I said, this can be tolerable or not, your choice."

"I don't see any advantage to being uncivil, at least for now. But...," Stacey states.

"Fine, you'll dine with me in the aft cabin. Your companion will eat with the crew, if he chooses to eat. Supper's at four bells during the evening watch. I'll send the sail maker to you. He can fashion something more suitable out of that dress for you. Four bells." He turns and strides aft.

Stacey skitters across the deck as the ship rolls and pitches in the swells. *Can't be much different than on the range, dirt verses water.* She watches the shadows on the deck, looks at the sun, clouds. *Due south, we're headed due south. What can I do to help my family find me? Can't leave any sign. What's Ocher always say? 'Trust your instincts.'*

Stacey lets go of the rail intending to walk toward the back of the ship. The ship drops in between waves lowering the front of the ship. Gravity takes affect and she slides forward. She gains control and grabs a new position on the rail.

One of the sailors pass by Stacey, "Morning, Miss, You'll get the hang of getting about after a bit."

"Thank you. Does it get any calmer the further south we sail?" Stacey asks.

The seaman just smiles, "I can't say, Miss. Not on sailing south or getting calmer. But no."

Be scared, be smart, stay mad and trust your instincts. They'll come for me. Be ready.

The days fall into the typical routine of travel, wake, bathe, eat, look at the sea, eat and sleep. After an all-night cry the first night she decides, enough of that. *I have to be ready when Dad and Ocher come for me. Crying won't help.*

Stacy catches quick glances of her companion, Terry. Abad and his companion seem to be ghosts. The pair don't dine with the captain or move about the ship. In the two weeks she's seen them only once. Her only concession to her captivity is making friends with the captain's cook. Not only to improve the cuisine but more importantly to try and obtain information that the man may have overheard.

One afternoon while preparing stew for the captain, Ivan, the cook, turns to Stacey, "Miss, I know that you're trying to use me to obtain scuttlebutt about our voyage. I don't mind that. Most of the crew does the same. I don't know much. Abad and his friend ain't big talkers and the captain knows better than to press 'em too hard. The one thing that the crew knows for sure is we're headed to Haiti. The only other thing that may mean something to you is the name 'Ocher'. He apparently has something they want and they're using you as bait."

"Thank you, Ivan." *Ocher? What does he have that they want? He'll come for sure. That could be a mistake on their part. Be ready.*

Chapter Thirteen

"Looks like someone's headed this way in an awful hurry," Bug says, pointing his hammer at the dust trail.

Ocher looks in the direction Bug's pointing. "Best be paying attention to where you're swinging that hammer. Let's get this corral stringer up, then deal with whoever that is."

"Ain't hit you but twice," Bug smiles in return.

Dusty, the new ranch foreman for the Double LL, reins up just short of the corral fence. His horse is all lathered up from a hard ride. "Ocher, come quick."

"What's up, Dusty?"

"Don't rightly know. Got a telegraph brought out to the ranch this morning. The boss sent me on the run."

"I'll get the horses saddled," Bugs says, as he turns toward the barn.

The three men ride up directly to the kitchen door where all the hands are standing or sitting around. Ocher recalls the same look on these men the day Woody died. No one speaks as he passes between the idling men and into the kitchen.

Amanda's crying and Lewis is pacing like a caged animal. He holds up what appears to be a telegram. "Stacey is missing," is all he can get out.

"What!" Ocher says. "How?"

"Nothing else, just more to follow," Lewis says.

Ocher reads the telegraph and confirms exactly what Lewis has said.

"It don't tell who, what or nothing," Lewis bellows at no one in particular. "When I get my hands on whoever touches my little girl..."

"Hey, boss. Someone's coming up the road," Dusty says, from the kitchen door.

"Maybe another telegram," Lewis says, stalking toward the doorway. "That's a wagon. Don't recognize the driver. See who it is and what they want," Lewis demands. "Sorry, Dusty. I'm a might occupied with other things. Take care of that will ya?"

"Sure, boss."

"I don't know what can be done from here, but whatever needs to be done will have to be done in New York," Lewis says, as he sits down.

Dusty comes back to the kitchen door, "Boss, it's a Texas Ranger and that other Ranger Holt. You best come out."

Ocher follows Lewis and Amanda out but can only see a slim older man holding the reins of the team.

"Ocher, back here," comes a familiar voice.

Holt is lying in the back of the wagon. "I'm sorry, Lewis, Ocher. I couldn't hold out."

"What are you talking about?" Ocher asks.

Before Holt can continue Amanda steps around Ocher and looks at the prone figure of Holt. "Lewis, Ocher, can't you see the man's in pain? Let's get him inside, out of the sun and out of that wagon."

Ocher extends a hand. Holt grabs hold and pulls himself to a sitting position. As Holt stands, Ocher steps alongside and Holt drapes an arm across Ocher's shoulders. Together they stagger toward the kitchen door.

Holt tries to continue, "They wanted you and then found out about Stacey. I had a letter. They want you and the jewels. I couldn't hold out. I'm sorry."

"We'll get to it. Let's get him inside. Lewis, have someone take care of that gentleman," Amanda says, looking back at the driver of the wagon.

"Dusty, take care of... sorry don't know your name," Lewis says, to the man in the wagon."

"Buck's the name."

Amanda says from the kitchen stoop. "Buck, you need any supplies, coffee, anything?"

"No need. I got what I need. If you can take Holt off my hands. Getting a might tired of his belly aching," Buck says, with a smile. "Besides I need to get back to El Paso."

"You sure?" Dusty asks.

"Yep. But thanks."

Lewis turns to Ocher, "Who wants you? What jewels and why Stacey?"

"Let's go in the house. It's time you all knew the truth," Ocher says, from the porch.

Chapter Fourteen

The kitchen's crowded. Amanda, Lewis and Holt are sitting around the table. Holt has been pillowed into Lewis' big chair, the one with arm rests. His cheeks are hollow and eyes swollen almost shut. The ranch hands lean back against the walls. Everyone has coffee but no one's drinking. In fact, it seems like nobody's breathing.

Ocher, after taking a big breath, starts to explain. "I was orphaned in the Philippines when I was five. I was taken in by what is called a Tong. This particular Tong trained their members to be assassins. That's what I am, an assassin," Ocher anticipates gasps and looks of distain from the assemblage.

Before he can continue, Amanda speaks up, "You may have trained that way but we know better. You're not that kind of man."

Around the room there are nods and statements: *Not any more. You're family.*

Ocher's breath catches as he tries to continue, "Thank you, but I was once. My first contract resulted in the death of a Japanese warlord. When I left, I stole a bag of precious jewels that the Tong wanted. It's expensive to maintain the training camp. I faked my death and kept the jewels. Somehow they've discovered I'm not dead and they want the jewels."

"I know how they found you," Holt says laboring to breath. "Remember just after you came into El Paso with the camels? You went to find a bath house and some new clothes."

"I remember."

"The old man heating the water asked you something in a foreign language and you answered him in the same language," Holt says, shifting in his chair trying to find a comfortable position.

"Yes, I spoke to him in Filipino."

"They were looking for you. There was a reward. He got the reward. He didn't know where you were going. We were seen together. My home base is El Paso so they found me easy enough. They ambushed me, kept me blindfolded and without warning, beat me with some kind of stick. I couldn't defend myself. No food or water. I don't know how long I was there. After they gave me the message, they dumped me. The stage coach headed to El Paso, stopped and took me in. That was four days ago."

Ocher looks at Holt, "First off, there's no way you could've stopped them from getting what they wanted from you. Most don't survive. You were going to be the hostage until they found the letter from Stacey. Now she's the hostage and you're the messenger."

Holt, with a great deal of effort, sits up. "Yep, Port au Prince, Haiti with the jewels. So when do we leave?"

The ranch hands leaning against the walls push off almost in unison. "Well, when do we leave?" Dusty asks.

Ochre looks around the room, "We aren't going. I'm going." He waits until the uproar dies down. "I'm also not taking any jewels. With or without the jewels they'll dispose of me. My only concern is getting Stacey back here safely. It's not a question of courage or riding for the brand. It's simple. I need to worry about me and not you. Please."

"Listen partner," Holt tries to stand, "I've got a little payback to administer, and I'm going with or without you. By the time we get to a ship and the voyage, I'll be fit."

Ocher just nods his head. "Fine."

"What's your plan?" Lewis asks.

"I need to send some telegrams. A friend of mine is in the shipping business. He may have a ship in Corpus Christi. I plan on leaving day after tomorrow and head to the coast. I'll stop by and have Doc come out to check on Holt."

"Lewis, I was going to tell you all of this before Stacey came home. If you didn't want me around I was going to leave and give you the ranch. After I get Stacey home, the offer still stands. I'll leave if you don't want me around your daughter."

"When you get back, and if I've read the trail right, I'll be glad to give away my daughter and I suspect that Ranger over there'll be your best man."

Ocher takes a drink of coffee because he can't speak.

Chapter Fifteen

The return telegram from Stanley Shipping comes back almost immediately.

Ocher
The Anna Belle is in Corpus Christi. You are part owner. Do as you wish. Captain Kacey is the best in the fleet. He and his crew await your arrival. What else do you need? Don't hesitate to ask.
C. Stanley

C. Stanley
I might have to take you up on the offer. Thanks.
Ocher

Ocher stops by the Double LL on his way back to his own ranch to check on Holt and tell him they have transportation. He finds Holt sitting in the front porch rocking chair cleaning Lewis's Greener shotguns. "I assume this is gonna be close-in action, thought these scatter guns would be more appropriate. I'm gonna get close enough to use 'em."

"I suspect you'll get your chance one way or the other. Stacey comes first."

"Goes without saying."

"You're in good hands here. I'll check in with Lewis and Amanda and head over to my ranch. A few things to tend to before we leave."

"Ocher, don't even think of sneaking off without me. I'll just follow you to Corpus and find a way to trail you."

"I know you will. What about the Rangers?"

"I'm on convalescence leave. I think that's what the major called it. He said come back when you're able."

"See you in the morning."

Ocher steps to the front door, knocks and opens the door. "Hello in the house."

"In the kitchen," Amanda replies.

She hands Ocher a glass of sun tea as he enters the kitchen. Her eyes red and swollen from crying.

"I'm sorry about all of this, Amanda. I'll get her back."

"I know you will and just as important, you come back with her."

"Mind if Bug and I ride the grub line for breakfast in the morning?"

"Anytime. Why not come back for supper?"

"I need to put some things in order but we'll be here at sunup."

Chapter Sixteen

Ocher and his foreman arrive well before sunup, knowing there had been no sleeping at either ranch. The house and bunkhouse lanterns show activity throughout the ranch. The aroma of breakfast draws all the work to a halt. As they arrive, they join the hands, headed to the kitchen.

"Morning, all. Looks like you got an early start," Ocher says, as he takes a vacant chair at the table.

Lewis smiles, "I suspect we got as much sleep as you did. We put things in order before we leave."

Ocher looks toward Lewis, "Leave? To go where?"

"With you. Now before you get all tied up in knots, we'll go just as far as Corpus to make sure you two get off ok. You don't want to leave that Pinto of yours down there for any length of time, so we'll bring him back. We might just hang around for a bit to welcome you home."

"Just you two?"

"Yep. The boys are more than capable of handling any ranch business for a while. So we're going."

Ocher smiles as he forks over another piece of ham.

They all look up when they hear the sound of an arriving rider.

A young gangly boy steps up to the kitchen door, "Telegram."

Lewis holds out his hand for the telegram, "Sit down and have some breakfast, Walter."

"Thanks, Mr. Livingston."

From the amount of food Walter gathers, it's apparent he doesn't eat very often.

Lewis opens and reads the telegram, then passes it to Amanda, who passes it to Ocher.

Mr. Lewis.

I have news about Stacey. Will arrive Corpus Christi at the Texas House by Friday the eighth. I will await your arrival until the fifteenth before I proceed.

Mrs. Barrington.

"How convenient," Amanda says. "Now I won't have to go all the way to New York," she pauses, apparently choosing to remain ladylike, "to discuss her lack of care for my daughter. Then I'll punch her in the nose."

The gathering all laugh, except Walter who's busy with his second plate of vittles.

Ocher looks over at Holt, "I've seen that look before. What is it?"

"Just a feeling. You might not want to punch her right away. Let her speak her piece. She wouldn't come all that way unless, well just unless," Holt says.

"I won't promise anything," Amanda replies. "More eggs, Walter?"

Chapter Seventeen

"**I** thought it was only ten to twelve days to Corpus. There's enough food in that wagon for a wintering," Ocher observes.

"Hush," Lewis says, as he steps up into the bench of the wagon.. "You never know. We might get weathered in somewhere. Besides, I don't want to go hunting for food."

Ocher rides around to the bed of the wagon. He decides to leave the Pinto at the Double LL. No telling where this journey will take him, or if he will make it back. Ocher hands Holt a money belt. "You might as well be useful. There's five thousand dollars in there," he whispers.

Holt tucks the belt under the blankets he's lying on and puts a Greener next to his right side and nods. Ocher notes that he's also wearing his Texas Ranger badge.

"Take care, boys," Lewis says, as he flicks the reins.

There's an established stage coach trail making traveling far easier than having to break a trail. Even so, by sunset the first day Holt is showing the effects of bouncing around in the back of the wagon. They camp for the night next to a creek. The water is cold and fresh. With Ocher's help, Holt heads downstream, undresses and sits in the cold water. Ocher can see that Holt's back and legs are covered in welts and bruises. Ocher has suffered through a beating or two that Holt described but nothing to the extent of Holt's mistreatment.

Supper is ready when they return. The cold water has eased the soreness of the day's journey. Holt seems to enjoy the meal but turns in early, making his bed next to the wagon and not in it.

Holt gets better day by day. He almost jumps out of the wagon on the eighth day when they arrive in Corpus Christi. He and Ocher enter the lobby of the Texas House to make arrangements.

"You must be Holt," says a rotund black lady. "So you must be Ocher. Just as Stacey described you. I'm Maggie. Mrs. Barrington's in there," she walks toward what appears to be a poker parlor.

Holt and Ocher follow but stop just inside the entrance. Maggie approaches a lady sitting at a poker table with four well-dressed men, her stack of chips much larger than theirs. Maggie whispers into her ear.

The women shuffles the cards with a well-practiced shuffle, a man's shuffle.

Odd, Ocher thinks.

The woman smiles, says something to the men, rises and approaches Holt and Ocher.

The lady is taller than Ocher's six foot, well dressed in a ornate black and lace dress. "Good afternoon, gentlemen. I am Julia Barrington." She starts to offer her hand, but stops. "You've met Maggie. Are Mr. and Mrs. Livingston with you?"

"Yes," Ocher replies.

"Good. Maggie, please tell the gentlemen we require the room and then make arrangements for our guests. And if you would be so kind as to have the chefs bring lunch in here."

Maggie nods and walks back to the poker table.

Lewis and Amanda are escorted into the room by a distinguished looking older black man.

"Thank you, Fredrick. Please see that we are not disturbed."

He nods, turns and closes the double doors as he follows the poker players out of the room.

"I am Julia Barrington," she says, looking straight at Amanda. "I take full responsibility for what has happened. If you will indulge me for a while I will tell you what I know and what I intend to do about it."

Amanda starts to step toward Julia Barrington. Lewis casually puts his arm around her shoulders to stop her. "Mrs. Barrington, I hold you completely responsible for this. Before this is over...." Amanda turns and walks out of the parlor.

Several men dressed in white uniforms enter the parlor, wheeling carts steaming with foods.

"Just leave it." Julia says.

"Is my daughter safe?" Lewis asks.

"I believe she is for the moment. I assume the kidnapping is for a ransom? When or if they get it, I... well, I don't know after that. Please, I have much to tell you."

No one moves toward the food. Seeing it as the distraction it's intended to be.

They gather around one of the poker tables, downwind of the aroma coming from the steaming lunch.

"My real name is Georgette La Beaux and I built this hotel and am still part owner. As a side note - you will be my guests while you stay here. Stay as long as you wish. This is not the first establishment I have owned or operated. The money for this enterprise was obtained while I owned a place in Port au Prince and I still have friends there."

"Mrs. La Beaux, are you trying to exact ransom as well?" Holt asks.

She smiles at Holt. "I am not married. The fact is I still have friends in many places, including the docks of New York. When Stacey did not show up for the graduation ball, I immediately suspected the Hightower boy.

There were rumors about the family's financial status. Fredrick spoke with his counterparts in the Hightower home. That led him to the docks. There are no secrets among the stevedores. There's a lot I don't know but I do know she was taken aboard a ship headed to Port au Prince."

"Port au Prince!" Amanda exclaims as she starts to stand. "That island. No respectable. My daughter. You allowed this to happen!"

Lewis places his hand on Amanda's arm. She sits back down.

Lewis looks at the lady across the table, "What do we call you, Barrington or La Beaux?"

"Georgette."

"Ok, Georgette, what were your plans if we hadn't arrived in time?"

"Simple. Go to Port au Prince and find Stacey and arrange to get her home."

"Sounds simple enough, Georgette, but we both know better," Ocher says.

"I'm missing something," Georgette turns to look at Ocher. "Why Stacey?"

"Hostage. They want me," Ocher says.

"Oh. So you're the cause of all of this," Georgette says, trying to deflect the anger of Amanda.

"Oh no, lady." Lewis states. This time Amanda places her hand on Lewis's arm. "You are responsible for her kidnapping."

Georgette chooses to remain silent.

"What do you know about those men who took Stacey?" Ocher asks.

"Not much really. They were described as pirates speaking Filipino. When I was in Port au Prince there was a camp on one of the outer islands that supposedly had a group of killers for hire. But that is just rumor. They were Philippine. Again that was the rumor."

Georgette stands, "I have things to arrange. Please excuse me."

"I think you better hear what Ocher has to say first."

"Ok."

"They're not killers for hire," Ocher starts. "They are members of a Tong trained in the art of assassination. We are trained in hand-to-hand, weapons, poisons, and tactics."

"We?"

"I was trained by that Tong as an assassin."

Chapter Eighteen

Georgette takes a long, hard look at Ocher. "You must be very good, for them to go to all this trouble to get you back. Or are they trying to get even for something?"

"Enough, Miss La Beaux!" Amanda exclaims, leaning across the table at Georgette. Lewis makes no attempt to calm his wife this time. "We entrusted our daughter to you and now she's gone. I don't intend to make nice with you and let you buy your way out of your incompetence. We'll pay our way and make our own decisions." Amanda straightens her dress and storms regally out of the dining room.

"She is absolutely right," Georgette says. "I make no excuses for my incompetence..."

Lewis interrupts. "Miss La Beaux, you best leave. My mother raised me to be a gentlemen. I wouldn't want to disappoint her. My wife said it quite well."

"But please, in some minor way let me help..." Georgette tries to continue.

"Lady, you are testing my patience." Lewis raises his tone a notch.

Georgette stands, pulls a kerchief from her sleeve and exits the room dabbing her eyes.

Fredrick re-enters the room, leaving the double doors open. "Gentlemen, it's apparently been an emotional meeting. Let me give you some facts to consider as you make your plans. The Barrington School has been sold. The proceeds of the sale were distributed among the staff. They were encouraged to seek employment elsewhere. The entire staff returned their payments when they learned that Miss La Beaux intended to return to Port au Prince to find and rescue Miss Stacey. In addition, the entire staff volunteered to assist in the endeavor. We all think a great deal of Stacey."

"Thank you for that information, Fredrick. But how can that help us?" Ocher asks.

"Excellent question, Mr. Ocher,"

"Just Ocher."

"Thank you, Ocher. To answer your question, most of the staff are from Port au Prince and the surrounding islands. No offense intended, but they'll blend in easier than all of you."

"Thank you, Fredrick. We'll consider the offer as we proceed. But, quite frankly, we don't have a great deal of confidence in you or your people," Ocher offers.

Lewis has been sitting, being unusually quiet, sipping his coffee. "We've never faced anything like this. Indians, rustlers, weather and drought we can and have dealt with. There can be no mistakes here. We'll consider every option that time allows."

"A reasonable approach, Mr. Livingston," Fredrick replies.

"Now," Lewis says, "can someone help me get my big finger out of this coffee cup handle? I got so mad I stuck my finger in there and can't get it out without breaking the cup."

Fredrick lathers butter on Lewis's finger and removes the coffee cup, "I will have the staff provide coffee mugs. I should have remembered Miss Stacey preferred a mug."

Chapter Nineteen

"**G**ood morning, sir. You would be Ocher?" The clerk flips through some papers.

"Yes, I'm Ocher."

"Message, sir."

The legend on the exterior of the envelope reads:

Stanley Shipping,
Front Street
Corpus Christi, Texas

Ocher:

We have three ships standing by for your use. I will be available to provide whatever you need.

Jorge Von Derr
Manager, Gulf Region
Stanley Shipping

The dining room is about half-full when Ocher arrives. Lewis is easy to find as he's the only white person in the room. As Ocher steps through the double doors he's met by a man he's seen with Georgette but has not been introduced to, "These are the men and women who would like to be involved in Miss Stacey's rescue. If you would permit me, I will introduce you to them. Each has a special skill that Miss La Beaux has made use of over the years. You might want to consider those skills."

"Certainly. Has Mr. Livingston been introduced?"

"He chose not to."

The man introduces each person and his or her special skill. Ocher thanks each one. He joins Lewis, noting there're no coffee cups on any of the tables, only mugs.

"Impressive group," Ocher says.

"Maybe. Sounds like a flim flam to me," Lewis says, as he pushes his plate back. "The grub looks good, but I ain't that hungry."

"This came this morning," Ocher says, handing Lewis the message.

"Do we need all these people and three ships?" Lewis asks.

"I don't know, yet. I'll know more when I talk to my friend Jorge," Ocher says, pointing toward the note.

"You know him?"

"He's one of Ollie's sons, the bookkeeper."

After a breakfast of Ocher's favorite, flap jacks, Lewis and Ocher follow the directions given to them to Front Street. The Corpus Christi building is almost a duplicate of the San Francisco building. A one story brick building, with the entrance door made of cargo hatches. The figurehead on the left side of the door is not a mermaid but everything else is pretty much the same.

"I am here to see Mr. Von Derr..."

"Ocher!" comes the bellow from the inner office.

Jorge Von Derr bends down to clear the door frame as all seven foot of him invades the room. "You've grown."

"Yep, sprouted a whole inch," Ocher retorts. "This is Mr. Lewis Livingston."

"Come in, come in, Mr. Livingston, I'm at your service. Anything. What can I do to help? The boss says anything you want," Jorge leads the way into the inner office.

"Before I begin, can your clerk be trusted?" Ocher asks.

"I trust him," Jorge replies.

So Ocher tells the story.

Chapter Twenty

"Man overboard," comes the cry from the main deck.

Stacey looks up from stirring the large pot of fish soup. "What's that mean, Ivan?"

"Someone fell into the ocean, Missy. Or jumped."

The ship heels over amid shouts of, "Lower the port long boat. Heave a line."

Almost immediately the ship rights itself.

"We didn't come about that quick, did we?" Stacey asks, exercising her meager nautical knowledge.

"No Missy, it would seem we ain't making any effort," Ivan answers.

The ship's captain storms into his quarters and slams the cabin door behind him. "Take her to her cabin Ivan and lock her in."

"Aye captain," Ivan responds, and gives Stacey an *I don't know* gesture, with his hands.

"Miss Livingston, to your cabin."

Stacey nods and follows Ivan to her cabin. In the last week, as land appears on the horizon, she's been confined to her windowless cabin.

"I'll be along about supper time, missy," Ivan says, as he closes her door and locks it.

She's confused about her confinement. She's adhered, for the most part, to her agreement with the captain about not trying to escape. *So why now?* The captain has tolerated her efforts to glean information from Ivan and the captain himself. She's acquired a good knife from the galley and hidden some hardtack, just in case the opportunity presents itself for escape.

Her cabin is stifling. The weather here, wherever here is, seems to always be hot and humid. She reflects that a cool bath or a drink would be refreshing. One thing is the same here. On the ocean, as in the desert, water is a scarce commodity. She receives a bowl full each morning to do with as she wishes. Bathing has become a non-necessity. What she wouldn't give to jump in the horse trough out by the barn. Twice during the weeks at sea, the ship encountered rain squalls. She enjoyed what the sailors calls a sea shower. A bath and clothing wash all at the same time.

Ivan tells her, "If you weren't on deck they'd all be down to their nothing and washing proper."

She's gotten her sea legs and she hasn't really been bothered by the ship's motion.

According to the ship's captain, "Your friend isn't fairing so well. A sailor he ain't."

She's seen Terry only three times. Each time he looked more gaunt and pale.

"Supper." Ivan motions toward the captain's cabin from the unlocked door. "Come along."

"Good evening, Miss Livingston."

"Evening, Captain Russell."

"Miss Livingston, let's dispense with the usual interrogation for this evening. I'm not gonna divulge any information about the voyage or destination. I do have some unpleasant news though. The gentlemen who came aboard with you went over the side this afternoon."

"What do you mean by over the side, captain?"

"We passed several leagues off an island. He came on deck, saw the island and dove over the side. I started to bring us about but was stopped by one of the paying passengers."

Stacey puts her hand to her face, looks at the captain, "Could he make it to the island?"

"Can't say. Even if he made it, most of the islands in this region are very inhospitable."

Stacey shakes her head and lowers her eyes, "I wish I felt sorry for him, but I don't. I feel sorry for his folks. Maybe one day I can tell them what happened."

The captain finally responds, "That would be nice."

Wanting to change the subject quickly, he says, "Weather seems to be approaching. I'd say by morning we could get a good wash down. Give us a chance to fill the water barrels. Could get a bit choppy, but you seem to be adjusting. If we get rain, I'll have Ivan escort you on deck."

"Why would I need an escort?" Stacey asks.

"More bad news. They, especially the taller one, seems concerned that you might try to escape, the same as your friend. I tried to convince him that you wouldn't try. He insists you remain in your cabin except for the meals. It's still my ship so for the moment, I'll allow you on deck if it rains."

"A sea shower would be nice. It's really too hot to eat. Besides I'm not very hungry. Would you please excuse me?"

"Certainly. Here, take an extra portion of water."

Stacey is awakened by the shouts coming from the main deck. "Rain! It's raining." She grabs the cloth she's been using to wash her face and a bar of lye soap and tests the door. It's unlocked. Ivan's standing in the passageway. The sun's just above the gunwale as she steps on deck. The rain's coming down in sheets. The deluge is warm and drenching. She soaps everything: clothing, hair, everything she can before the rain stops.

The ship's bosun yells, "Ye had enough of a soaking. Now get them barrels in place under those rain catchers. Step lively, mates."

The entire deck aft of the main mast is covered in soap. The men are skating about with the barrels. It doesn't take long in the rain until the deck's rinsed clean of the soap.

She glances to the starboard rail and sees two of the Philippine men washing. The taller of the two men has his back to Stacey and has his shirt off. A seaman, moving one of the empty barrels into place, bumps into the shirtless man causing him to turn and face Stacey.

Her world is turned upside down. She can't breathe. She wants to move but can't. Finally, she forgets the rain and rushes from the deck to her cabin. She sits on the edge of her bunk crying. It can't be. It just can't. The tattoo on the man is the same as the one on Ocher.

Chapter Twenty-One

"Morning, Holt. You're up early," Ocher says, as he enters the dining room.

"All the commotion woke me up."

"Yea, I heard some myself," Ocher says, filling his coffee mug from the pot sitting on Holt's table.

Holt looks up from his gravy and biscuits. "The La Beaux crowd pulled out last night."

"All of them?"

"That's what the note says. The clerk gave me the message this morning." Holt hands Ocher a folded piece of paper.

To whom it may concern:

We have booked passage on a ship leaving for Port au Prince. The ship changed itinerary at the last moment. No time to discuss departure with you. We will learn location of Stacey and any additional information by the

time you arrive. Will reimburse your expenses
when you arrive.

G. La Beaux

Ocher puts his coffee mug down on the table without even taking a sip or sitting down to join Holt.

"Ocher, you thinking what I'm thinking?"

"Something sure ain't right about this whole thing. You seen Maggie or Franklin recently?"

"Nope."

"Stacey sure set store by those two. Now they seemed to have disappeared," Ocher says as he stands.

"Or deserted," Holt adds.

"That would be consistent with Stacey's appraisal of the two, but why? Holt, you hang around here. I'm going to ask around a bit. Tell the Livingstons what you know."

Ocher's first stop is Stanley Shipping. "Morning, Jorge. Got a minute?" Ocher asks, as he enters the office.

"Yes, I was just about to send for you."

Ocher doesn't waste any time, "The La Beaux crowd, did they sail this morning?"

"Yes, but..."

"But what?"

"Ocher, I can't absolutely prove any of this, but I'm pretty sure. You always told me to trust my instincts."

"And what are your instincts telling you?"

"Well, the supposed destination of the *Gallant*, that's the ship that they sailed out of here on, is Port au Prince. Not likely. She has no provisions for that trip. All the provisions their captain ordered are still sitting in the chandelier's warehouse. I checked about half an hour ago. I don't know where she's headed but it ain't Port au Prince."

"Why did you check, Jorge?"

"Instinct. There's some chicanery going on here. I just don't know what it is."

"If you had to guess..."

Jorge starts to speak, stops, starts, stops and finally, "They're waiting for you to sail tomorrow and then doubling back here to pick up the supplies. After that I don't know. Those supplies are bought and paid for. The *Gallant* is or was scheduled for England."

Ocher sits quietly. The only sound is the ship's clock as it ratchets away the seconds. "Jorge, you know anybody in New York? Someone you trust?"

"Yes. Fellow I went to college with."

"Let's me and you send some telegrams."

Chapter Twenty-Two

Ocher finds Holt at the same table engaged in pretty much the same activity as their previous meeting. Eating. "This your new hobby?"

"Got to keep my strength up. I got some scores to settle."

"Yea, I know. That's what I wanna talk to you about."

"I seen that look before, Ocher, and I don't think I'm gonna like what's coming next. Spit it out."

"Holt, I need you to stay behind."

"Hold on, cowboy. I didn't ride all the way down here in the back of a wagon just to stay behind."

The apple pie was now being ignored.

"It's important, Holt. You know I wouldn't ask if wasn't important."

"OK. Let's hear it."

Ocher spends the next half hour laying out his information and finally delivering the conclusion. "Think I'm wrong?"

Holt leans across the table, reaches for the pie, pushes it away and leans back in his chair. The grandfather clock chimes in the background as Holt leans forward again. Finally. "When I was engaged in the war, we had this kid from back east. He traveled around with his family doing a magic act. He once told me that they really didn't do magic, just misdirection." The clock chimes again. "I'll do what you ask, Ocher. Just between you and me, I get seasick anyway."

"I could be wrong. I'm not telling the Livingstons any of this before we leave."

"Aren't they staying here until you get back?" Holt asks.

"Would you stay here if this happened to your family?"

"Not likely. So you sail tomorrow on the tide. I'll leave tonight, just in case someone might be interested in following me. I'll gather some friends along the way. Ocher, my friend, I led a pretty reasonable life until you came along. Glad you did though."

"One last thing, Holt. Watch your back. 'Leave no witnesses', is a way of life for the Tong. You, my friend, are a loose end and a witness."

"I'll manage."

"Then there is this La Beaux person. She isn't right."

"I been a lawman most of my life, Ocher. I have put away a lot of evil folks during that time. If your friends want my scalp, well... they'll have to stand in line. Especially La Beaux," Holt responds, reaching for his pie.

Chapter Twenty-Three

There's been no sleep for the last two days. Stacey's mind wrestles with what she thinks she knows and what she actually knows. *He can't be like those men, but he can do things no cowboy can do. He is responsible for me being here. Why? Is he coming to rescue me or.. ?*

The knock on the cabin door interrupts her mental free-for-all. "Missy, wake up. Get your belongings together. You're going ashore," Ivan says from the passageway.

Just after the evening's eight bells, the ship's motion changes. From the commotion on deck she guesses that the crew is taking in the sails. Then she hears the call of the bosun to set the anchor. She believes she'll be leaving the ship. Ivan only confirms her fear.

Stacey hears the key turn in the lock. Normally she would consider that sound as a prelude to freedom, but not now. She knows, or suspects, she's going from a prison that she's tolerated, to one she can't even guess about.

"Time to go, missy," Ivan says, as he opens the cabin door. He won't look at her, he just points toward the bow. "I suspect they'll search you and your gear, missy. Hope you hid those knives real good."

Stacey tries to smile but can't. "I did."

There are longboats being lowered on both the port and starboard sides. Foodstuffs mainly but bundles of goods that she can't identify are being loaded into the boats. The shorter of her captors walks over to her, grabs her right hand and affixes a shackle, then does the same to the left. Without speaking, he points to the rope ladder draped over the starboard rail. She hesitates just a fraction of a second before being pushed to the rail.

Ivan is standing at the rail and says something but the pounding in her ears, from her heart, drowns out his words. The usual sounds from the crew are absent. She hopes they realize what they've done and remorse sets in to save her. It does not.

The ocean is silent as well. The only sound is the oars as they penetrate the sea. She can smell the vegetation from land and the odor of the cargo in the boat. Dried meat, spices, burlap, molasses and sweat, the sweat from the oarsmen and her own sweat of fear. She considers going into the ocean but knows she has no chance of survival in the water.

"There," is the only word spoken, as the little man points to a torch on the beach.

The helmsman adjusts his course to head toward the light, the only light on the moonless and silent night. *This can't be Ocher's doing. It just can't be.*

The oarsmen ship the oars, bring the oars to the inside of the boat, as the bow nudges the beach. The two in the bow step over the side and push the boat further onto the beach. Her captor points then waves toward the side of the longboat.

"I'm not getting in the water."

"No speak. Get out."

"No."

He starts to reach toward Stacey when one of the oarsmen offers his hand, "Here let me help you."

"No help."

Before the little man can move to stop Stacey's gentleman helper, the three oarsmen from the other side of the longboat step up behind the man, "You best stay seated or you'll be wearing an oar across your bow."

The little man turns and glowers at the men but stays put. Stacey is carried ashore and set on the dry sand. "Sorry miss, we all are, but..."

From the interior of the beach several black clad men immerge from the darkness. "Just unload the cargo on the beach. We'll take it from there."

The helmsmen of the longboat, the ship's bosun, steps up to the man speaking English.

"You want it on the beach, then you put it on the beach. We ain't stevedores, mate."

Stacey watches as the oarsmen silently pull the longboat into deeper water.

Immediately there's a verbal confrontation with several of the black clad men speaking to the English speaking one, who's trying to argue with the bosun.

"All right, all right we'll unload the boats."

Stacey's seen four longboats on the ship and assumes they're all here on the beach loaded with cargo.

"All right, you seadogs, unload the cargo," the bosun bellows.

The sound of splashing is heard as the goods hit the ocean. The sea is filled with bundles of drifting cargo. Before any reprisals can be made against the men from the ship, the longboats are gone.

The English speaking man walks over to Stacey, "This way. Stay close. There's snakes."

Stacey smells the smoke from wood fires long before she sees the camp, the aroma of the ocean long gone. Her fear has eroded her ability to judge time. It could be one hour or many more since leaving the ship.

"You sleep there," the English speaking man points. "You might want to wait 'til daylight before trying to escape. I'll save you the effort. You can't escape, but try if you must." He walks away.

Stacey looks at her appointed sleeping area- a raised platform covered in leaves with a canopy also of leaves. Only one other time in her life has she been this afraid. *At least back then I had a gun and I understood the enemy. Indians.* She sits on the edge of the platform just as a tremendous flash of light invades the darkness. The light's followed by thunder. *That sounds like an explosion. The ship, the men, Ivan.*

From across the camp, in the darkness, "Leave no witnesses."

Chapter Twenty-Four

Ocher walks into the dining room. He's greeted by a very resolute looking Mr. and Mrs. Livingston, sitting at the table closest to the door.

"Morning, Ocher. With all of that commotion keeping us up, Gave me and Amanda time to talk. We've made a decision." comes from Lewis.

"Morning, Lewis, Amanda. What's on your mind?"

"We're going with you and Holt and that's that," Lewis says.

"Ok."

"What do you mean ok?"

"Ok. You and Amanda are going with me. We leave at eleven this morning, on the tide. You'll be going. Holt is staying. I have some things to tell you. But not here. Get your things together and we'll take them down to the *Anne Belle*. Then we can walk over to Stanley Shipping and have the privacy we need."

In the lobby, standing among the few pieces of luggage, Ocher settles the bill presented by the clerk.

Lewis looks at Ocher with a puzzled look, his brow all furrowed, "I thought La Beaux said..."

"Later Lewis. We need to just leave."

The three of them don't need assistance loading the luggage into the rented carriage before climbing in. "The *Anne Belle*, pier six," Ocher tells the driver.

The *Anne Belle* looks to be just as gangly as she appeared the first time Ocher saw her in Japan. "She ain't pretty, folks, but she can hold her own in a swell on the bow or abeam."

Pier six is set off from the main commerce piers and warehouses, making it a bit tougher to observe the comings and goings of passengers and crew. "Wait here. We'll be back directly," Ocher tells the driver.

"I been paid for all day," he responds.

Ocher grabs his kit bag and walks up the gangway with Lewis and Amanda. At the head of the gangway he stops and looks aft to the bridge deck. "Permission to come aboard?" He directs to the man standing watch.

"Granted. I'll inform the captain."

A voice from forward of the main mast, "Good morning, I'm Captain Kacey. Welcome aboard," offering his hand. "You must be Mr. and Mrs. Livingston and you are Ocher Jones."

Ocher observes that Captain Kacey looks like a man who has sailed the seas. Six feet, broad shoulders, stanchion straight back and green eyes that sparkle with mischief. The offered hand reflects years of working with ropes, sails and rigging.

"Mr. Stanley speaks highly of you and he isn't easily impressed. He's made it very clear. Whatever you need, I'm to make available if at all possible."

"Thank you, captain. To be honest about it, I don't know what I, we, will require," Ocher responds, as he shakes the very healthy grip of the captain.

"Not to worry. My crew and I are quite capable both at sea and ashore. I'll have your gear stowed in your quarters. Mr. Von Derr is aboard and requests your company in my cabin. Please join us for coffee or tea."

Ocher hails the buggy driver, "We're staying aboard. You can leave."

The driver gives a salute gesture and snaps the reins.

Ocher notes that the condition of the *Anne Belle* reflects the pride of the captain and crew. The teak decks shine from scrubbing with soap stone. The hand rails, stanchions and ships wheel are laced with fancy rope work. The mooring lines are coiled in concentric circles on the deck. This is not the *Anne Belle* of Captain Quarte.

Chapter Twenty-Five

Captain Kacey leads the group aft toward his cabin. As he opens the door and escorts Amanda into the space, Jorge Von Derr stands to introduce himself. All seven feet.

"Oh my," Amanda looks up as she accepts Jorge's hand.

Lewis stops dead in his tracks in the doorway.

"I get that a lot," Jorge remarks, as he shows Amanda to a chair at the captain's table. "Mr. Livingston, Ocher."

"Hello, Jorge. We intended to come over to your office. This saves us a trip," Ocher says, as he steps around the table.

"Captain, how soon can we sail?" Jorge asks.

"We?" Ocher says.

"Yes, we. I'm going as a representative of Stanley Shipping."

"We?" Ocher says again.

"Ocher, you've got a lot to learn about family." Jorge looks defiantly at Ocher.

"We can be underway in just over an hour," Captain Kacey interjects, "Ocher, you can try to stop him if you want, but not me. I'm just the captain here. So if you'll excuse me, I'll make appropriate arrangements for sailing the fleet on the tide."

"Fleet?" Ocher asks.

"We have three vessels all provisioned ready to get underway. Don't say anything, Ocher. We have legitimate business to take care of at Port au Prince. We'll just have some additional resources if we need them."

"We?" Ocher repeats.

"Ocher, if Dad needed you, where would you be?" Jorge asks.

"At his side?"

"That's right. Dad would be here if he could, but he can't. In fact that whole tribe would be here if I asked. They couldn't get here in time. So you get me. That's how families work."

"That's right, Ocher," Amada chimes in. "Get used to it."

"All right. I just hope I can keep you all safe."

"We been keeping ourselves safe long before you came along, Ocher. No different now, just a change of scenery," Lewis offers. "I know you got more to say, Ocher, but I want to see how this thing gets away from the dock. We have time to hear the rest. Especially why Holt ain't coming."

Chapter Twenty-Six

Captain Kacey turns toward Lewis, "Question, Mr. Livingston?"

"Lewis, please, Captain, and yes. It appears that the water is high enough for us to sail across. Why are we waiting?"

"As a matter of etiquette, Lewis. While on deck, Captain is appropriate. In private I am 'Swen'. You asked an excellent question about the tide. The incoming tide is about to turn. We'll have a pause known as slack tide and then the tide will recede, or go out. Typically, in this port, when the tide turns and recedes, the wind follows the tide. We'll move away from the dock using a stern spring line. That'll bring our bow into the tide and we sail with the wind and tide at our stern."

"You make it sound easy, Captain."

"If you train your crew properly and they trust the training itself, it's easy. This crew's been trained properly. Just as important, I respect them as seasoned sailors should be."

The *Anne Belle* clears the harbor and immediately encounters the swells coming in from the Gulf of Mexico. Lewis attempts to leave the bridge deck but stumbles down the stairs. A short, stout man grabs Lewis before he falls completely to the deck. The sailor appears to be built like a tree stump. Lewis bumps into him and confirms he's as solid as a stump.

"You'll get your sea legs under you soon enough. The swells come in a pretty regular manner. You'll get the rhythm. I'm Turner, the ship's bosun. No worry, by the time we make Port au Prince, I'll be making you an adequate sailor."

"I'm Lewis and I hope so."

The bosun strolls off across the ship's deck as if it were a dance floor, never missing a step. He would nod or point to a piece of stray gear that needed attention and immediately a seaman would make it fast or stow it properly.

Lewis doesn't stroll. He holds fast to the gunnels or any other solid object. Just as the last bit of land melts below the horizon he solos and makes a hands free approach toward his quarters. "Amanda, how come you ain't wallowin' around like I am?"

Amanda smiles, "Remember that old mule, Tess? It's just like riding her and that gait she had. Once you got the sway right. Besides that, my legs aren't bowed like yours. It's a wonder you can walk at all. Ocher asked me to gather you up and come to the captain's quarters.

Chapter Twenty-Seven

Lewis follows Amanda to the captain's quarters. The Captain, Ocher, and Jorge are sitting around the table.

Ocher looks around the table and finally states, "I wish I had a plan to ease all of our concerns, but I don't. At least I have no solid plan for rescuing Stacey, not yet anyway. But to answer your earlier question, Lewis, 'Where is Holt?' Holt is on his way to the Double LL."

"Our ranch? What or how could these kidnappers figure into the ranch?" Lewis asks.

"They don't. La Beaux figures into this, in a big way."

"There's always been something that bothered me about that woman," Amada says, "Just couldn't put my finger on it. This just keeps getting worse," Amanda says, with a quiver in her voice.

"Yeah, me too," Ocher continues. "After La Beaux introduced us to her crew, I noted that the page where we all signed in was torn out of the book at the front desk. Maggie and Franklin disappeared and then the message about leaving without a reasonable explanation and reimbursing us when we get to Port au Prince, got me thinking."

"Reading trail sign? Where'd it lead you?" Lewis says, as he reaches for the coffee pot.

"I went to Jorge and we sent some telegrams to New York. The answers were very revealing."

"I'll say," Jorge pushes his coffee mug toward Lewis.

Ocher continues, "La Beaux didn't sell her business. They just left. The school had major financial problems. In fact the Pinkertons are looking for the whole bunch."

"I see where this is goin', I think," Lewis pours Jorge some coffee.

"The brutal fact is, and I am speculating here, La Beaux figured we would be killed by the kidnappers, leaving the ranch unprotected." Ocher takes a deep breath and looks around the table.

"I really don't care about the ranch right now, just Stacey," Amanda starts to cry. "You're one of these animals, Ocher?"

Outwardly Ocher doesn't react, but inside he feels gutted. "I was trained by them, yes. They are skilled and ruthless. They leave no witnesses. As soon as the opportunity came to escape, I did."

"No witnesses," Amanda whispers," Does that mean...?"

Ocher hesitates and finally looks directly at Amanda, "Yes. Their plan is to eliminate any and all as soon as they get the jewels."

"You think Stacey's still alive?" Amanda asks, through her sobs.

"Yes, absolutely. She'll remain relatively safe until I rescue her. I will return her to you. I promise."

"How?" Lewis asks, trying to hold back his own tears.

"I have the beginnings of a plan. I have a distraction."

"How?" Lewis asks again.

"I will return her to you, I promise. When I do, you can take her home and you'll still have a ranch to go back to."

"Let's be realistic," Lewis offers. "They couldn't just move in and take the ranch. The ranch hands wouldn't stand for it."

Amanda stands and looks toward the galley, trying to regain her composure.

"They could if you willed the ranch over to them after your death," Ocher counters.

Amanda stops and turns back toward Ocher, "Our letters and the signatures in the ledger. They have handwriting for Lewis and me. Yours as well, Ocher."

"Yep. That's why Holt is headed to the ranch with some Texas Rangers and Pinkerton agents."

"Your plan is for you to get Stacey out safe. What about you?" Lewis asks.

"I promise to get Stacey out and Holt will keep the ranch safe. Right now that's all I can promise."

Jorge looks at Amanda, "Well, that's not quite all of it."

Ocher glances at Jorge, "What do you mean, that's not all of it?"

"Remember when I said Mom and Dad couldn't get here in time?"

"Yea, I remember."

"The whole crew, including my big brother, is headed to Texas to help."

Ocher drops his head and folds his hands on the table, "It would appear that the La Beaux gang is about to be introduced to the most lethal weapon I know. Marta's kitchen spoon."

Chapter Twenty-Eight

Stacey's still sitting on the side of the sleeping platform when the sun comes up, too afraid to sleep, think or move. In the dawn, she can see a half dozen men around the camp. Some are sleeping, while others are talking as they unpack the cargo parcels from the ship. She can't understand any of the language being spoken.

She's startled, when from behind her, "If you want to eat, you must cook for the camp."

Stacey stands to face the voice, "I won't cook!"

A man of oriental appearance, smaller than six foot, black eyes and black hair, is facing Stacey. "We will not feed you or let you to eat. You cook, you eat. You cook, you get fresh water. You no cook, maybe the jungle feed you. Go, look, then come back and cook."

The men working with the cargo bundles stop, watch the exchange with no reaction.

Stacey doesn't want to concede anything to the man but does want to scout her surroundings and to plan her escape. She turns and walks out of the camp.

All night sitting on the side of her sleeping platform, her mind won't stop. *What would Dad do? Do I trust Ocher? What would Ocher do? Leave no witnesses. One thing both Dad and Ocher have said is, 'Trust your instincts'. Ok, what are my instincts telling me? I don't know.*

Stacey remembers *English*, as she calls him, warning about the snakes. She treads softly, in her bare feet, through the sparse vegetation, carefully watching for snakes or anything else. The ground is sandy, the air is thick but clear, it's warm and she can smell the ocean. The vegetation gives way suddenly and she's standing on a beach. She can see to the horizon from her right and to the left. She sees nothing but ocean.

Stacey notes her shadow's position, to her right. The sun is on her left, east. The beach is oriented east and west, something she didn't know. She decides to walk west with the sun at her back. I'll mark this spot and walk 'til noon then turn around. That way the sun won't be in my eyes.

This early in the morning the sand and the water are the same temperature on her feet. The vegetation is to her right about one hundred feet away. She can hear birds and insects but no human sounds.

The ocean reveals nothing. Slowly the shadow being cast by the land mass creeps over her right shoulder. The longer she walks, the more the shadow grows. And the more she realizes her predicament. She continues her reconnaissance. The shadow recedes but her fear grows. Her dread is confirmed when she reaches the pile of debris she used to mark her starting point. She's on an island with no other land in sight. Now she understands. English has no concern about her escaping. There's nowhere to go.

Sitting here watching the ocean doesn't achieve anything. Stacey hikes back through the trees and up to the camp. She can hear conversation but can't understand the words.

"Satisfied?" English asks. "Ready to cook?"

Stacey ignores him. She can see that one of the pigs, that was brought ashore in a long boat, is being butchered. She's seen this type of activity many times. What does catch her attention is the big green object being hacked open. During her walk she saw them all over the beach.

One of the men husks the object like you husk corn. He then takes a small pointed knife and drills a hole in the thing and drinks from it. After breaking it open, he pries out some of the white interior and eats it.

"Yes," English says behind her, "You can survive on coconut but only for a short time. The fruit prevents scurvy."

Something about the coconut is on the edge of her memory but she can't touch the thought. She turns away from English and starts back toward the beach.

During her first walk she noticed that the coconuts were almost everywhere, except one small stretch of beach. *Why not there?* She returns to her original marked starting spot and walks the opposite direction. Only this time she walks in the water, the surf erasing her footsteps. As she comes to the barren stretch of beach, she remembers. *Look for sign. Dad taught me when something's different, look for the why.*

She slows her walk, looks and listens. It's a small sound, the sound of a bird that stops her dead in her tracks. *There're no meadowlarks out here.* Her heart is thumping to the point she can't hear another call. She turns in the direction of the first melody. There, standing in the vegetation, is Ivan.

Ivan puts his finger to his lips to signal silence and turns and walks into the vegetation. Stacey looks around to see if she can see or sense anyone watching her. She picks up a large dried leaf and brushes away her trail.

"Hello, Missy."

"Ivan. How did you get here? Is anyone else with you?"

"I'm alone. I don't know about the rest of the crew. They was kinda drifting the other direction. You ok, missy?"

"I'm ok for now, but ..."

"Don't cast about for evil, missy.   We'll figure something out. Best keep your routine. I been shipwrecked before. I'll manage. How did you find me?"

"No coconuts on the beach."

"Should've known, being raised on the range and all. Your pa teach you to look for sign, did he?"

"Yep."

"You done good, missy. I won't make that mistake again."

"How do you get into that thing?" Stacey asks pointing toward a coconut.

Ivan picks up a coconut and walks over to a lava rock. The rock has a natural point and he jams the husk onto the point. After several attacks the green husk's loose enough to peel. He picks up a sliver of rock and drills into one of the natural depressions of the nut. He hands the coconut to Stacey, who drinks as she saw the men do.

"Not bad. Not as good as spring water, but not bad."

"Keeps a body alive. Now just bash it against the stone to break it open and use the small piece of rock to pry out the fruit."

Stacey smiles at Ivan, "Now I won't have to cook for them. At least for a while."

"They want you to cook for them?"

"Yes. 'No cook, no eat', the one man says."

"Perfect, now we have a plan," Ivan says, with a big smile.

Chapter Twenty-Nine

"You'd think after all this time I'd get used to this low hanging equipment," Jorge says, rubbing his head. "I must walk into some nautical thing a dozen times a day. Ain't meant to be a sailor."

"To be honest about it," Ocher responds, "I'd much rather be sitting on a horse. At least if you fall off you can walk. Believe me it's much easier to walk a mile than swim one."

"I see you been talkin' to the crew. They help with a plan?"

"Yes. Everything hinges on where they're holding Stacey. I know her captors and how they think. It has to be on an isolated island so they can observe any ship approaching. According to a couple of the crew there are several possibilities."

"In a big ocean, several is a tall order."

"I agree. There's a few weak spots in their planning."

"What?"

"Communication, transportation and escape."

Ocher waits as Jorge mulls over his statement. "That's why Dad always turned to you in a tactical situation."

The two men take time to appreciate the moment. The sound of the wind in the sails, the sea brushing past the hull and the sound of the ship's bell, signaling the change of afternoon watch. Knowing the drastic changes to come.

"How do they tell those on the island you have arrived? How do they leave?" Says Jorge, after a pause, "There has to be a ship waiting in Port au Prince."

"You seem to have left out a possibility, Jorge."

"I didn't leave it out, I was just avoiding it."

"Kill me upon arrival and take the jewels. Either way that doesn't help Stacey, does it?"

"I see only one logical solution, Ocher. Don't arrive."

"That's what I was thinking. We have to find the ship they plan on using. I believe I can convince them to provide the location of the island."

"There you go with the 'I' again, Ocher Jones. You can't go into port, plain and simple. You have to trust someone else right now. I'll have the captain hail the other ships so we can confer. You'll stay on the *Anne Belle*. There are fifty good men on those other two ships, men I trust. I'll sail out on one of them and we'll find what we need to know and go from there."

"But, Jorge..."

Jorge, who had been gazing out to sea, turns slowly and looks down at Ocher. "You'll sink under the load you're trying to lug around. Look around man. You expect people to trust you with their lives and the lives of the people they love. Where's your trust? We didn't come along for the entertainment or watching you probably get yourself killed. We don't need a martyr, we need someone to lead, who has faith that there're those around you that are quite capable. More importantly to trust us."

Ocher smiles, "Thank you, Jorge. I needed to be reminded of all of that. Let's go meet with the captain and the Livingstons."

Chapter Thirty

"Can you hold out for a day or two more, Missy? Don't want to give in too easy. That will give me time to do some fishing."

"I think so. The one that speaks English said I could probably hold out with coconuts for a day or two. Fishing?"

"Yep, Puffer fish. I'll explain if'n I can catch some. You go about your walks and such. You got a keen eye, you'll see my trail. You best be goin'."

"Thanks, Ivan. It's good to have you here."

Stacey takes a different path back to the beach, erasing her footsteps with a palm frond. Using the leaf as an umbrella she steps into the small waves breaking on the beach and continues her walk.

She returns to camp carrying her palm frond and the coconut she opened. She places the nut and stone sliver on her sleeping platform.

"You get tired of coconut quick. You will cook," English says, as he eats what smells like rice and pork from a bowl using his fingers. "Smell good, is good. You will cook."

Stacey does like the aroma of the dish but ... *I have to stay alive. I know they'll come. I can't poison them without poisoning me. Ivan, I hope you know what you're doing.*

Just after sunset the heavens open up and the rain persists for two days. She's hungry and the rice and pork begin to smell great. She learned aboard ship, if you get wet in the tropics the humidity keeps you wet and cold. Stacey decides to remain close to her small shelter and stay dry during the rain event. Water's not a concern but food is. She's ready to relent and cook, but first.

Finally the rain relents. Stacey takes her palm frond, stone knife and heads to the beach. She walks in the waves looking for a sign. It's a small thing but enough, a shell lying on top of a coconut. Walking inland she erases her footprints.

"Knew you'd see it," Ivan says.

"You doing ok, Ivan?"

"Don't care for raw fish much, but keeps a body alive. Drinking water ain't been a problem. You ok?"

"I'm hungry, so I guess I'm going to cook. Don't want to, but need to stay alive until..."

"No need to fret, Missy. You come from good stock. They'll be a comin'. There'll be hob to pay when they get here I suspect. This Ocher fella, is he one of 'em? Don't make no sense holding you, to get to him, if he's one of 'em."

"He's got a tattoo like them. I don't know, Ivan. I hope not."

"He rich or something? Heard something about jewels."

"Don't know. I just don't know."

"Well, Missy, time to make our play," Ivan walks over to a small glass bottle with a twig stopper stuffed into the neck. "Don't worry none about gettin' it on you. Might sting a bit but won't kill you. If'n you eat or drink it, well that's a different kettle of fish."

"When I cook, I'll have to eat and drink what they do. But I know a way."

Chapter Thirty-One

"Sail ho," comes the cry from the top of the main mast.

The captain strolls to the wheel deck and looks through his telescope, "It's the *Oleander*. Bosun, strike the sails. Stand by for her to come alongside."

Before the bosun can give orders the hands are hauling in the sheets, keeping just enough canvas aloft to maintain steerage.

"I thought I'd never get sick of water, but..." Lewis says, as he looks toward the approaching ship. "Now maybe we can get on with it."

The seas are almost dead calm allowing the *Oleander* to approach and be hauled into the *Anne Belle*. As the lines are made fast the captain of the *Oleander* is piped aboard.

"Captain Harper, welcome aboard," Captain Kacey offers, looking at Harper's bandaged hand.

"Thank you, captain. Minor disagreement. Quickly resolved."

"Sail ho," from the main mast.

"That would be the *Argentine*, under the command of Captain Jorge Von Derr."

"Von Derr, a captain? There's no *Argentine* in our fleet."

Captain Harper just smiles, "I won't steal the man's thunder. With your permission we'll fleet up and parley when the good captain arrives. A favor though."

"Certainly, Harper. What is it?"

"Pipe Jorge aboard. It will please him."

"Aye, Captain Harper."

Jorge Von Derr steps over the port rail of S/V, sailing vessel, *Argentine* and onto the main deck of the S/V *Oleander*. Immediately the trill of a bosun's pipe announces the arrival of a ship's captain. Jorge can't smile wider. He swaggers across the deck and steps over onto the deck of S/V *Anne Belle,* where honors are again rendered. In an effort to maintain his composure, he leaves the deck taking his giant steps aft toward the captain's quarters.

"I didn't know what to do first time honors were rendered," Captain Kacey remarked.

"Neither did I," Captain Harper follows.

In the captain's quarters Ocher, Kacey, Andrew Harper, Jorge and the Livingstons settle in around the table.

"All right, Captain Von Derr, tell your tale," Captain Harper says, holding the chair for Amanda.

"I appreciate the honors, but your crew, Andrew, did the sailing. I got to watch and get called captain."

"What happened? My daughter is out there." Lewis almost yells.

"We found the ship hired by your associates, Ocher. We also found the location of the island. The spy left behind to spot you, well... he won't be joining them."

"Then we can sail there and rescue Stacey?" Lewis says, his voice raising an octave.

"Lewis, let's hear Jorge out and then take appropriate action," Amanda says, placing her hand on Lewis's arm.

"Yes, dear." Lewis replies, knowing better than to raise his voice at Amanda.

Jorge continues, "We went ashore and spread out in the taverns. After buying a fair amount of grog, tongues began to loosen. One of our crew found the ship's company that was waiting for Ocher. So we converged and bought more ale. After a bit we had to carry the men back to their ship. Once aboard we overcame the rest of the crew. There was a Philippine guy on board who apparently knows what Ocher looks like. Don't know if he was supposed to grab you or just report to the island. I've seen what his kind of training can do, so when he came at me I shot him. We locked the rest of the *Argentine's* crew in a cargo hold and sailed."

"They still in the cargo hold?" Ocher asks.

"Yep, had a talk with their captain though. He got real talkative when threatened with keel hauling. That was Captain Harper's idea."

"Ocher, there's nothing in Port au Prince that we need. No use to keep the other ship moored there. So, I've sent the *Lantana* here," Captain Harper says, pointing to an island on the chart lying on the table. "Stacey is on this island," again pointing to the chart. "This island is far below the horizon of Stacey's island. We'll not be seen. Both islands are well off the trade routes. We can be there by sunset tomorrow."

Ocher takes a pair of calipers to measure the distance, "And I can be on the island by the time the sun comes up the next morning, with a little help."

Chapter Thirty -Two

Stacey walks back to the camp site with several coconuts held in her arms. She places them on her sleeping platform and rolls down the cuffs of her worn canvas pants.

"More coconuts?" English asks. "Not ready to cook. I not ask. You cook. Now."

Stacey sits on her platform, folds her arms and looks straight into English's eyes. "No."

English steps forward and grabs Stacey by the hair and drags her off the platform. "Now."

"All right, all right. I'll poison you if I get the chance."

"We watch. No poison. You eat first."

Rice and pork are not staples on the ranch, but she's observed the other men cooking and if they can do it, how hard can it be? She adds spices and fresh vegetables to the pork and cooks the rice separately. In addition she finds the ingredients to make biscuits, her secret. She is watched every second by one of the men with Ocher's tattoo. She signals English with a wave of her hand that the meal is ready.

English walks over, picks up a bowl, and fills it with rice and pork, "You eat."

Stacey is hungry. "My pleasure." She accepts the bowl and reaches for a biscuit. There are no forks or spoons in the camp. She devours her meal. Taking the biscuit she rubs in around the inside of the bowl to get all of the gravy and every last morsel. "May I have some more?"

"Go, sit. You done for now."

Stacey walks back to her sleeping platform to watch the men. Sure enough every one of them use the biscuits.

"Go wash bowls, there," English points to a porcelain pan filled with water.

Stacey complies and gives the bowls a *thorough washing.*

The nights are always quiet. After the camp settles in you can hear the surf and the buzzing of the insects. During the day, the only real sounds are the men practicing hitting each other. At least that's what it looks like to Stacey. I miss the sounds of birds. There're no birds here, just a few passing, squawking seagulls.

The morning meal is just reheated from the day before. "Make biscuits," English demands.

Stacey is all too happy to comply. The evening meal is much the same. Stacey eats from the pot as she prepares the food. Even offering English an occasional taste from her spoon. Guinea fowl, spices and biscuits are served in a *washed, clean bowl.*

Chapter Thirty-Three

The S/V's *Anne Belle, Oleander, Lantana* and *Argentine* are moored around what's been named Captain's Island. The small patch of sand is so named because you can't spit without splattering a captain. The only lights showing are below decks. Any light might shine against the clouds.

Earlier the fight had been settled. Those who wanted to go to Stacey's island would've required sailing the entire fleet, probably losing the concept of surprise. After much heated discussion, it's decided that two long boats will be deployed, one boat with Captain Kacey and Seaman Lusk. The other vessel is to be manned by Turner and Ocher.

"Perfect night for a little sailing wouldn't you say?" Captain Kacey offers, as he limps across toward his assigned boat.

Ocher notices the limp, "You ok, captain?"

"Just fine. Storm coming in a day or two though. Need to get about our business."

With each oar stroke Ocher can feel his apprehension level rise. *I'm as good as or better than anyone in that camp, I hope. Get Stacey and get out. Then, what? I'm the cause of all of this. Will I become just a wanderer like Abel or will I find....?*

"There she be, dead ahead. You ready, Ocher?" Turner asks, shipping his oar.

"Yes."

"Over the side with you then. Two hours, right here."

"Yes."

Ocher slides into the water. His feet hit the sandy bottom. The water is chest high and the temperature about the same as the air. He tries to calm his breathing. The only thing he can hear is his heart beat in his ears. *The next two hours. Is this what fear is? Fear of what I might find or might not find.*

He fights the friction of the water, stopping at ankle depth, listening. Nothing. One step, stop, one step, stop. The clouds must be moving but he can't tell, no moon. One step, stop. Something's wrong. He moves back into the water and alligators down, head and ears above the sea. *Did I hear something? Just wait. Can't wait, two hours.* Stand, one step and then another.

The vegetation is sparse, but not the insects. *If I was here I would camp on the highest point.* Ocher moves, barely lifting his feet, feeling every twig, *Make no sound.* The wind's at his back so he's not surprised that he can't smell a camp fire. He can see about fifty feet. The volume of insect buzz increases. *Odd.* He moves forward. The sparse vegetation ends. The camp is within his fifty foot vision. Typical sleeping platforms, full, at least most of them. The insects, no fire. He backs away.

It's a small thing, actually two small things. The smell, *It's death, no doubt, but who?* The second thing is the sound of bare feet moving on the sand, behind, outside my field of vision. *Two hours.*

Where would I put Stacey? There, over there away from everything she could use as a weapon. Ocher melts back away from the smell of the camp and moves through the trees to a sleeping platform he hopes is Stacey's. *Empty.* He feels around the surface, nothing. Not even the smell of death. He backs away.

That sound again, bare feet, off to the left. *Time to introduce myself.* Ocher decides to make his way back toward the beach and come up behind the bare feet. *One hour.*

It's a tall lanky man who steps out from behind a tree. Ocher has him pinned to the tree with a knife pressed to his throat.

"You must be Ocher," the man squeaks. "Stacey's gone."

"Gone? What do you mean gone?" Ocher increases the pressure on the knife.

"English took her and sailed off in a ketch he'd hidden."

"She all right? How long ago? Who are you and who is English?"

Ocher eases the pressure but keeps his knife in place.

"English, that's what she calls the only one of those yahoos who speaks English."

"She's safe? You're sure?"

"Don't know about safe but she was ok last I saw. By the by, I'm Ivan."

"How long ago did they sail and in which direction, Ivan?"

"Two hours at most. Fella didn't strike me as knowing much about the sea. I suspect he's got the wind at his stern and headed norwest."

Ocher stows his knife between his shoulder blades and grabs Ivan by the arm dragging him toward the beach. "English wasn't alone was he?"

"No. They was seven more besides him. The rest is dead. Missy managed to poison them."

Ocher stops and looks at Ivan, "Poison them? How?"

"Good question. Let's get after them and when we catch up, we can ask her."

Ocher realizes the implication of the insect humming in the camp. Seven dead can draw a lot of interest. He continues toward the beach, Ivan in his wake.

"Ahoy in the boats," Ocher yells toward the ocean.

"Ahoy," comes the return.

"Come ashore."

Two long boats materialize out of the darkness and are maneuvered to the beach. Kacey, Lusk and Turner step into the water and rush to Ocher.

"Who's that?" the captain asks, pointing toward the tall man standing behind Ocher.

"Ivan. He was with Stacey."

"Where's Stacey?" the captain continues.

"English, one of her captors, took her and sailed away about two hours ago."

Captain Kacey looks at Ivan then at Ocher, "Ivan, what kind of boat? Two hours you say? With a storm brewing a smart man would head in only one direction, northwest with the wind astern."

"That's how I figured it, sir," Ivan recognizing a seasoned sailor when he sees one. "They're in a single masted ketch. I don't know how well provisioned."

"It won't matter how well they're provisioned when they get caught in stormy seas in a sloop." The captain says, as he considers his next move. "Ocher, you and Ivan get back to the *Anna Belle* with Lusk. Turner and I will sail after English and Stacey. Lusk you tell..."

"No captain, you take charge of the fleet. Turner and I will go after Stacey."

"Mr. Jones, I do not intend....."

"Captain Kacey, I'm an owner of those vessels and I've made my decision. You, sir, are the man I want taking charge of those vessels and the crews. Is the bosun capable of taking up the chase?"

"Turner's as capable as I am, Ocher. We'll be several hours behind you. Turner, Port Isabel would be my port of choice. I don't know if this English fellow has a plan or is just trying to escape. The barrier island east of there, well you know, there's no way off.   You have water and hard tack. God Speed. Lusk, Ivan, let us be gone."

Chapter Thirty-Four

"Captain Ocher, no disrespect, but before I get volunteered, I prefer to be asked."

"I'm sorry, Turner. Do you want me to hail the captain and ask one of the others?"

"Hell no. I'm glad to be considered capable, especially by that captain. If we survive this, you owe me at least one pint of ale, of my choice."

"Done, but don't call me captain. What I know about sailing is that I know nothing about sailing. Is there anything we should scrounge off this island before we leave?"

"Probably, but we don't have time. I'll manage the sail and we can take turns at the tiller."

Ocher and Turner push the long boat off the beach and set the sail. In a matter of moments they're making headway. The seas are relatively calm as the sun rises at their backs.

The island is just off the starboard quarter, "There, I think I see the head of the truck, top of the mast, on the ketch," Turner relays, pointing almost straight ahead. "She's a bit bigger with more sail but we're lighter. When the swells increase, they'll have the advantage. Keep a steady hand, man."

At local apparent noon Turner scuttles to the stern, "We ain't making much progress, mister. You trust my judgment, Ocher?"

"Yes, what's on your mind?"

"You been holding steady on that ketch dead ahead. I want you to shift the tiller slightly and hold that truck just to the starboard side of the bow. I'll make a mark for you to steer by."

"Won't that take us away from them?"

"It'll appear so. I'll trim the sail and we'll gain speed. If we wait, the wind in the coming storm will tear us apart. It's now, later won't do. If we can get abeam of them we might be able to out maneuver them. Have to bet on me being a better sailor than he is. The rest is up to you."

"Make your mark, captain."

Turner smiles, accepting the compliment.

The day wears on. The heat and humidity aren't diminished by the wind. The sun has climbed and receded. The monotony of the waves against the hull bring promises of sleep. Ocher can see the upper half of the sail in the ketch, but no one in the boat.

"I'm going to get a bit of rest. When the moon rises, hail me," Turner calls aft as he curls up in the bow.

Ocher's hands and arms are sore from gripping the tiller and he wants to rest, but he

knows that if the weather worsens Turner will
need to take the tiller.

"Turner, yo Turner," Ocher shouts forward.
"The moon."

The bosun looks aft then over the starboard
gunnel, "Well done, mister. We even gained on
him in the last four hours. I'll take the tiller. You
get some rest. Eat some hardtack and have some
water. By morning the weather will hasten our
decisions."

Ocher has no stomach for the hardtack but
gags down a wafer and takes on some water. The
deck's hard and unforgiving, the seas are
dancing about but neither stops Ocher from
dropping instantly into sleep.

Chapter Thirty-Five

"Ocher, Ocher wake up man," Turner screams, "She jumped over the side. Your woman's in the water."

Ocher's first reaction is to jump in the water and swim to Stacey.

"Stay in the boat man," Turner yells. "We don't need two of you in the drink. That other fella's sailing away. I'll come about downwind of her. That way she floats toward us and we don't float over her."

Every muscle in Ocher's body wants to jump in the water, but he trusts Turner. The sea is Turner's domain.

Stacey rises with the waves, looking around for the trailing boat. She locates the vessel with the two men just before dropping into the trough between waves. *Ocher, that looks like Ocher.* As she crests the next swell, she waves. The man in the bow waves back. *That's Ocher.* She drops into the trough again.

"Watch your head. We're coming about," Turner says, as he points toward the boom. As the boat, the boom swings across the boat. If Ocher hadn't been warned, the swinging sail would have knocked him over the side.

"Stand by to grab her, starboard side," Turner points to the right side of the boat.

Ocher leans out as far as he can and grabs Stacey under her arms. Her entry into the boat's not elegant but efficient.

"Watch the boom. We're coming about again," Turner again points, as he turns the boat.

Stacey, wet, scared, relieved and grateful, grabs Ocher. They tumble to the bottom of the boat in a mass of soaked clothes, wet hair and hugs. "I knew you'd come for me. I saw your boat, so I jumped," she says, into Ocher's ear.

"Of course I did. Along with half of west Texas. We'll talk later. Right now we have a bigger problem. That storm," Ocher says looking astern of the boat. He'd point but he has both arms around Stacey.

Turner tries not to look at Stacey. The wet clothes cling to her, "Ocher, there's a small piece of canvas stowed forward. For her," Turner yells, and points. With the wind picking up, pointing seems to be the best means of communication.

Ocher retrieves the canvas and wraps it around Stacey. "It ain't much but it'll keep the wind off you. Turner," Ocher tilts his head toward the man steering the boat, "says it's gonna get a lot worse."

"Don't care," Stacey says looking into Ocher's eyes, "I'm here and with you. We'll manage."

"Hate to interrupt you two," Turner yells, "but I need to trim the boat and sails. Can't do it alone."

Ocher reluctantly releases Stacey and crawls aft toward Turner.

"Just hold steady. I'll check the gear. I'd say the worst of it will be just after sunrise. Just about time we get to the outer barrier island," Tuner yells.

Ocher struggles with the tiller but keeps a steady course until Turner returns. "I think I can man the tiller if you want some rest," Ocher tells Turner.

"Won't be no rest for anybody, but you can hold steady until it gets dark. By that time, we'll be bailing the water out," Turner responds, unfolding several canvas buckets.

The night collapses on the boat. First it's day and then it's night. Turner relieves Ocher at the helm and Ocher starts forward.

Stacey has given up trying to stay dry. She arrived wet and nothing has changed, especially now with seawater coming over the bow and blowing in from the stern. In addition, only about half of what she's bailing out of the boat with the canvas bucket gets thrown overboard. The rest she's wearing.

"Sorry mate, you can't go forward to her. Too much ballast forward. Stay amidships and aft of her and start bailing. Use the canvas buckets. She already has one," Turner points.

Ochers' arms are aching but he keeps bailing. He feels a tug on his pants leg.

"I can hear the surf breaking. We're just offshore of the barrier island," Turner yells into Ocher ear. "It's gonna take a bit of luck to get ashore. You have to man the sail."

Ocher nods.

"When I give you the down signal, you lower the sail. When I give the up signal, raise it again."

Again Ocher nods.

"If we capsize, use the bucket as a float. Turn it upside down, fill it with air and hope. One way or the other we'll get washed ashore. Tell her. Good luck."

Nod

Ocher creeps forward, cups his hand over Stacey's ear, relaying the information about the bucket. She looks as frightened as he feels.

She nods and reaches out and squeezes Ocher's hand.

He smiles his best reassuring smile.

Ocher stations himself at the sail and watches Turner for the signal. Ocher can feel the boat rise on a swell just as Turner gives the down signal. Ocher drops the sail. Amazingly they ride the top of the wave until it breaks off shore of the island. Just as the boat's engulfed in the froth of the wave, Turner signals up. Ocher raises the sail. The rest of the ride isn't smooth but the boat and its occupants sail right to the beach. Turner gives the down signal. Ocher drops the sail.

Turner jumps out of the stern into the water and motions for Ocher and Stacey to get out and help pull the boat up the beach.

"If we can get this boat over the high point of the island and turn it over, we'll have a little shelter." Turner yells at them, as they pull the boat. "We could try and use the sail and let the wind push the boat but that's too risky. We'll just have to lug the thing."

After what seems like hours of pushing, pulling and fighting the wind, water and exhaustion, the boat's on the lee side of the island and has been turned bottom up. The sail's been taken off the mast, the mast un-stepped. The three climb under the boat and cover up with the sail.

The blowing wet sand assaults every small opening until the voids are filled. The trapped air is stifling.

There's no use talking. The wind and rain assault the boat, making communications impossible. Not all communications. Stacey's huddled up against Ocher, resting in the crook of his arm. Ocher's head is lying on hers. Turner's just plain jealous.

After several hours of enduring the barrage of the storm, "We've got a decision to make," Turner yells. "Two things are gonna happen. One: it's gonna get dark. Two: the eye of the storm is gonna cross over us or close enough over us. When it does, we could sail over to mainland. Either way we still have another half of this storm to go through."

"What's the advantage to moving?" Ocher asks.

"We'll have to move anyway. The storm will come from this side of the island once the eye passes, putting us on the windward side," Turner responds.

"I don't want to get back in that boat unless I have to," Stacey adds.

"When this storm passes, where's the easiest place for the ships to see us? Here or on the mainland?" Ocher asks.

"Here," Turner responds. "But there're no provisions out here. Fresh water's out of the question. We'll have firewood and some washed up fish."

"Can't we get fresh water in the buckets from the rain?" Stacey asks.

"Good question. No way to keep them from collapsing unless you stand out in that and hold the bucket open. That wind's blowing around everything that's loose. In the dark you wouldn't see a tree limb or jetsam coming at you. Not worth the risk."

"Would it be a long walk to civilization if we go over there?" Stacey asks.

"We may have a guest either place. Don't forget English," Ocher adds.

"Never," Stacey says, in a voice that cuts through the noise of the wind and rain.

"Let's move the boat to the ocean side when it gets calm and stay here for the duration of the storm. If we get lucky, the ships will find us. If they don't, then we can sail to the mainland. OK with you, Turner, Stacey?" Ocher asks.

"Fine by me. Don't get too comfortable. We'll need to move quickly," Turner huddles back under the canvas sail.

Stacey nods her approval.

The wind doesn't diminish, gradually announcing the arrival of the eye of the hurricane. The wind just stops.

"It's time," Turner announces, as he unfurls from the canvas and digs his way out from under the boat. He walks to the highest point of the sand dunes to determine the best place to move the boat.

Ocher and Stacey join him.

"Finally some fresh air," Stacey remarks, taking in a deep breath. "You can even see the moon."

"It won't last long, Miss Stacey." Turner points toward a small patch of greenery just west of them. "Looks like the best place. That vegetation should hold the dune in place. I hope."

The three return to the boat and start the task of push, pull and drag. They can see the opposite side of the eye wall approaching just as they get the boat settled in. Ocher takes a long measured look before joining Turner and Stacy under the boat. He doesn't see any sign of English.

There's no gradual increase in the wind. It just attacks.

Just as the howling begins, "It's gonna be worse than before. We're on the northwest side of the storm..." Turner starts to say, before the wind and rain drum him out.

The intensity of the storm is frightening. Not only the wind and rain but sand. The wet sand blows over the crest of the dune and piles up against the boat making the air in the interior of the little shelter almost too dense to breath.

Ocher sticks his head out from under the canvas sail and can actually hear Turner speak in a normal voice. "About over mates. Give it about an hour and we can crawl out of here. The sun should be along shortly."

"You think it's safe enough for me to go out right now?" Ocher asks.

"Worried about that English fella?"

"Yes."

"Still gonna rain a bit. Might wash some of the sand and salt off all of us. Might as well try. The flying loose stuff isn't much of a worry," Turner replies, as before digging his way out through the sand.

Stacey follows. She stands, spreads her arms and then washes herself off in the rain. Ocher and Turner follow her example. She finishes her shower by combing her hair with her fingers and then smiles at Ocher.

"What did you mean about half of west Texas?"

"Well," Ocher begins, "Your mom and dad are out there on a ship. At least I think they are. A friend of mine from San Francisco is with them. There are four ships and about one hundred crewmen, minus one. Turner volunteered to come with me. Your friend Ivan is also onboard one of the ships. Holt and the Double LL hands are guarding the ranch from Miss La Beaux and company."

"Mom and Dad on a ship? On the ocean?"

"Yep. Your dad should stick to ranching. A sailor he ain't. Your mom, not too bad."

"Who is Miss La Beaux? At the ranch?"

"Barrington's real name is La Beaux," Ocher says. There's a lot more to this. The rest can keep for now."

"Ocher Jones! La Beaux, Barrington and the ranch?"

"Short version. La Beaux thinking maybe we all get killed out here and she could waltz in and take over. Probably sell it quick and move on. "

It's too dark to see Stacey's reaction. She just reaches out and takes Ocher's hand. "I'll want the whole story, soon. But it sounds about like half of west Texas helping. I've got a lot of people to thank when we get home."

"Yep, me too. Turner, if you had to guess, how far east of us would you say English sailed?"

Turner's voice comes from the pre-dawn light, "If he managed to stay afloat and make land fall, he probably is five or more miles from here."

"A determined man could walk that pretty quickly and could be on the way here now," Ocher remarks.

"Maybe," Turner continues, "There are a few shallow inlets east of here. The storm could have closed them or opened up new ones."

"When do think the sun will come up?" Ocher inquires.

"Two hours more or less," Turner answers.

"If you two want to get some rest, I'm going to stay up, just in case a determined man shows up," Ocher says, walking to the crest of the dune. Stacy and Turner follow.

Chapter Thirty-Six

With dawn come the insects.

"Miss Stacey, I know you don't want to get back in that boat. But, if we stay here the bugs gonna eat us alive." Turner swats a mosquito on his arm.

Ocher stands and holds his hand out to assist Stacey. He thinks, *If I was in the jungle I would know right where to go to get leaves to rub on as repellent. Not much jungle here.*

"Will it be any better in the boat?" Stacey asks Turner, as she still holds on to Ocher's hand.

"If we stay here, Miss, we'll have to deal with mosquitoes, sand fleas, little biting things, thirst, hunger and the sun. On the boat, with a bit of breeze, we won't have to bother with some of those inconveniences," Turner answers.

"You have any idea where we are?" Ocher asks, looking up and down the estuary.

"Well, sir, I'm pretty sure we are on Matagorda Island. Approximately fifty miles from nothing," Turner responds. "Let me think on that a bit. Corpus Christi is that way," Turner points to his left. "I think. Port LaVaca may be closer."

"What's in LaVaca?" Stacey asks.

"Rough place. Been there once, was glad to leave," Turner shakes his head.

"Stacey, you ready to get back in the boat?" Ocher turns to face her.

She nods. "What about Mom and Dad? How will they find us?"

"Miss Stacey, those ships out there are manned by the best sailors in any fleet. The old man, the captain, knows the sea. Your folks might've been bothered a bit but they're fine. The captain will find a way to use the ships to cover as much water as possible. If he figures four ships ain't enough, well, he'll engage everything that floats in the Gulf to find you," Turner says, with obvious pride.

"Looks like it's still mighty rough out there," Ocher says, looking out toward the sea.

"We'll stay on the bay side. A little less wind but a lot more comfortable." Turner walks toward the boat. "Let's heave this thing over the dune again and get her into the water. See if she floats."

After Turner declares the boat seaworthy, he and Ocher step the mast and rig the sail. Stacey gathers up the canvas buckets and extra sail.

"Well, that's about as shipshape as it's gonna get. We'll cast off and see how she's gonna sail. Might have to shift you two around to maintain trim," Turner says, as he takes command.

The small vessel catches the wind. Turner steers to the middle of the bay, staying out of reach of the clouds of mosquitoes and other bugs. The heat rises with the sun.

"Ocher, lower the sail," Turner says. "We're gonna rig that extra sail to block the sun. If we don't, we'll cook."

Turner supervises every move, assuring no one falls over the side. The canvas does block the sun but does nothing to decrease the humidity and heat. What little breeze there is, is no help at all.

They continue to sail through the bay. From their position, they can see trees that have blown down. The rivers and creeks are cascading into the bay. It's fresh water but undrinkable. Slowly civilization debris starts to appear.

"Tide's going out and we must be getting close to some port. That flotsam looks like it comes from buildings," Turner gestures forward, the direction they're sailing.

"Look, there's a table," Stacey says, pointing to a floating object with four wooden legs in the air.

The flotsam level increases, "Must be getting pretty close to something," Turner says, as he navigates around the debris. "There," he points. "That's La Vaca or what's left of it. Getting supplies will be tough, but we can try."

There are ships sunk at what appear to be docks, boats ashore, skeletons of warehouses, and in the distance, parts of structures. Here and there are small work parties sifting through piles of what used to be La Vaca.

Turner beaches the small boat on a sandy spit of land outside the natural harbor. He and Ocher step out and pull the boat further ashore.

"Is that you, Turner?" asks a bearded man. Even at a distance it's apparent that a bath and clean clothes are needed. The disheveled man's carrying a bottle of spirits in his left hand.

"Hello, Mickey," Turner responds, his voice not indicating the two are friends.

Mickey eyes the three voyagers, "Come ashore for supplies? Don't see much in that there skiff."

"That's right, Mickey. Any chance of getting some fresh water and food?"

Mickey says immediately, "You wait right here. I'll fetch you water and food. Don't leave. Might take a wee bit of time. Don't leave."

"That was too easy," Stacey remarks, stepping out of the boat.

"Your friend, you called him English, is already here," Turner says, nodding in agreement with Stacey.

"Yes, I think you're right," Ocher says. "What do you suggest, Turner?"

"Well, I know what I'd do. I'd bring the water first. Make an excuse about the food to keep us here. I'd go back into town to find English expecting a reward."

"We need the water," Stacey says. "I can go a little longer without food."

"Turner?" Ocher asks.

"Makes sense. Let's see if he brings anything," Turner responds.

"I'm going to move over there in the shadows of that pier, just in case he brings back English and not water," Ocher says, and points to a collapsed section of pier.

Turner and Stacey retreat to the shade of the sun screen. Turner takes the time to check the tiller, mast and rigging of the skiff. Stacey bails some water to keep busy.

"Turner, a little help here," Mickey yells, rolling a small cask with his foot and carrying a smaller one.

Turner meets Mickey and takes over rolling the larger cask. "You didn't think to bring a cup, did you?"

"No. I brought you my empty instead," Mickey holds up the empty bottle. "Where's your friend?"

"Around. Needed some privacy."

"Oh, yea, sure."

"I'm gonna pour a drink for me and the lady. Any food?" Turner asks, as he sets the small cask on the upturned larger cask.

"Couldn't carry it all. I'll need some time to fetch it. You stay put, get some water and I'll be back," Mickey turns. Ocher's standing there blocking his path.

"Mickey, I thank you for the water. I'll pay you for it with a word of advice. The man who's looking for us has no intention of paying you for the information. He'll reward you by killing you. He makes his living at it."

Mickey looks at Ocher and then at Turner.

Turner nods, "We've never been ship mates Micky, but you're still a sailor like me. This other man will kill you without any thought on it."

"But Turner, he showed me three twenty dollar gold pieces....."

"That's as close as you'll get, Mickey. Seeing it," Ocher says. "Probably the last thing you'll see."

"I don't know," Mickey says, eyeing the boat and the three occupants as they push the skiff back into bay.

Mickey's still standing and watching as the small boat rounds the harbor entrance and sails out of sight.

"Miss Stacey, hope you weren't telling a tale when you said you could do without food," Turner says, passing the water bottle back to Stacey. "We be about fifty miles from Corpus. We won't make it today. Tomorrow for sure."

"I'll be fine. How about you two?"

"Been hungry before. Probably happen again. I'll manage with the water. At least it's good water," Turner says, as he steers around a floating tree.

"I'll be fine," Ocher says, accepting the water bottle from Stacey. "Turner, what about tonight? We going to have to deal with bugs?"

"Maybe some. We'll find a place to anchor off shore from the island. That'll cut down on some of them. Won't be the most pleasant night you've ever had. But we've been through worse," Turner replies.

"You think English will sail after us?" Stacey asks Ocher.

"No, I don't think so," he responds.

Stacey remains silent for a while, "Yes, I agree. Seems to me that he got to shore somehow and walked or stole a horse to get to La Vaca ahead of us. He sure didn't sail past us."

"Good thinking," Turner says, from the stern of the boat.

"So, he'll figure out pretty quick that the only logical place for us to go is Corpus," Stacey continues. "He'll probably get there first and be waiting."

Ocher smiles, admiring the logic of Stacey's thinking. "There's one thing he doesn't know about, though," Ocher says, and waits for Stacey to puzzle it out.

"Ivan, the cook," she says, smiling. "He knows what English looks like. But English doesn't know Ivan. If Mom and Dad get to Corpus before we do, Ivan can identify English."

"That's right," Ocher says.

Turner has a big smile on his face. The look seems to say, *That's one smart young lady.*

The floating debris diminishes and the sailing, although slow, continues through the afternoon.

"Look lively crew, we're going ashore just there and retrieve some of those rocks," Turner says, pointing toward the island. "We can load them into the buckets and use them as an anchor for tonight. If we wait, well, just about sundown the mosquitoes will eat us alive."

Turner beaches the skiff. Ocher and Stacey each grab one of the canvas buckets. Immediately they're discovered by the insects.

The buckets are loaded into the boat. "Let's go over on the seaward side and see if there's anything washed ashore we can use," Turner says, headed over the dune.

The three of them swatting at flocks of buzzing, biting insects as they cross to the windward side of the island.

"What's that?" Stacey asks, pointing down the beach.

"Supper," Turner answers, running toward the object on the beach.

Stacey and Ocher catch up to Turner. He's holding onto a sea turtle, the turtle trying hard to return to the sea, legs just a-paddling, wriggling, "We'll have to endure the bugs for a while but sea turtle's mighty good," Turner says, holding up the turtle. "There's more of a wind on this side of the island. Should keep the bugs down while we roast this thing."

"Want us to gather some wood and get a fire started?" Stacey asks.

"Good. I'll get this ready for roasting," Turner responds.

Ocher and Stacey return, carrying dry wood. Ocher reaches into his pocket and brings out his rock sling. "I'll get a fire started," he says as he starts to make a friction bow.

Stacey watches both Turner and Ocher. After she sees that there'll be a fire and something to cook, she walks away to find more firewood.

"I still prefer beef," Stacey says, after two helpings of turtle. "But this isn't bad."

"Yes, it'll do," Turner says. "Best we get off this beach before sunset and find a place to anchor."

Ocher stands and helps Stacey to her feet. They both kick sand into the fire pit and follow Turner to the boat.

"Perfect," Turner says, as he points just to his left. "That's an old inlet that the storm closed in. It's got sand bars on both sides and we can anchor in that little false lagoon. Tide won't make much difference and no other boat can sail over us. Stand by with the anchors."

"You think we're safe here, Turner?" Ocher asks.

"I think so. Stacey's right, English will try and get ahead of us in Corpus. There ain't no weather about. Ships can't sail on the back side of the island. The sand bars shift too much. We're as safe as we can be. No need for a watch. Besides, Ocher, I never seen anybody sneak up on you yet."

The sun screen is removed. There's a breeze blowing from off shore over the island keeping the majority of bugs at bay. The canvas is spread over the gunnels and the three retreat to the canvas cave. Turner is in the stern with Ocher and Stacey huddled together in the bow.

After settling in, "The stars are just as bright and plentiful here as at home. I prefer dry land," Stacey whispers to Ocher.

I prefer anywhere you are, Ocher thinks to himself.

Ocher is startled awake.

"It's just me, Ocher. Had enough sleep. When Miss Stacey wakes up, we can set sail. Time to get you two on some solid ground," Turner whispers to Ocher, trying not to wake Stacey.

"I'm up," Stacey says, sitting up and folding the canvas cover off her.

"Well then, let's have some breakfast of smoked turtle and lukewarm water. Then set up our sun screen and make sail," Turner announces.

The turtle meat is cold and the water warm but they're glad to have both.

"Weigh anchor," Turner commands his crew.

They both stare at Turner.

"Pull up the bags with the rocks. Then dump the rocks overboard," Turner points toward the water.

"Will we make Corpus Christi tonight?" Stacey asks.

"We should, miss, mid to late afternoon. But don't get your hopes up on much being there. You seen La Vaca. Could be worse in Corpus or not as bad. Much bigger place and folks will be scrounging around for necessities. I wouldn't count on any of the fleet being moored yet either," Turner answers.

With the prevailing wind out of the west, Turner can't set a course running with the wind. They tack across the bay to make headway. The debris from Port La Vaca is left behind but trees and other natural debris have to be navigated around.

In the late afternoon, "Smell that?" Stacey asks.

"Yep," Turner says. "A lot of produce comes into Corpus and gets held on the pier in warehouses. Smells to me like the warehouses didn't stand up to the storm too good. The stuff's rotting in the sun."

Ocher's been silent most of the day thinking about English. "What would you say, about an hour?"

"Maybe less, but soon. By now we should be seeing the tops of ship's masts," Turner observes, looking in the direction of the odorous rotting vegetation. "Most likely they all set sail to weather the storm out there instead of getting smashed against a pier. Or dragging an anchor and getting blown inland."

Turner navigates the small boat through the debris. The stench gets stronger and the mass of floating garbage gets bigger. Turner steers the boat through a small opening on the west side of the harbor and beaches the boat. "This's fresh water. Not drinkable but fresh. You two stay here, I'm going ashore. You'll be safe here." He doesn't wait for an argument, just disappears up the river bank.

Ocher scouts around their area, assessing the defensibility of the place and a way to escape if necessary.

Stacey steps into the water, takes a hand full and smells it. Deciding it isn't tainted, she starts to wash her arms and legs, getting the salt and sweat off.

Just at sunset Turner returns with six men. "These are mates of mine. We've sailed together, bunked together and fought side-by-side. I trust them. Miss Stacey, you won't be going nowhere without at least two of my shipmates going with you."

Stacey considers telling Turner she's quite capable, but with English out and about, she says, "Thank you, Turner."

"Ocher, he's here somewhere. Scuttlebutt is there's a reward for you two. I'm offended that I ain't included in that reward, but I'll get over it," Turner says, watching Ocher look over the men. "By the way, guard duty makes a man mighty thirsty. Whenever your ships moor up and the Captain takes over the guard duty, you're buying."

"Only if you join in," Ocher says smiling.

"That'll be up to the Captain, if he can spare me for that long," Turner says, with a wink.

Chapter Thirty-Seven

"That's mighty fine food, Miss Stacey," Vincent says, holding out his bowl for another portion.

Stacey smiles, "Vincent, you always seem to come in last from guard duty. Why is that?"

"Just to make sure none of your cooking goes to waste."

Over the next four days, the small camp settles into a routine. During the day there are three guards on the perimeter of the camp, one with Stacey at all times. The other two are with Turner and Ocher in town helping the clean-up, gathering supplies and watching for English.

As Ocher, Turner and the two seaman are returning to the camp, Turner points toward the gulf. "There. On the horizon."

"I see something. What is it?" Ocher answers, looking where Turner's pointing.

"It's the top of a ship's mast. There's a pennant flying. It's one of yours. That's the

Stanley Shipping Pennant. One of the ships has arrived."

"Turner, is there any way to signal the ship before she comes into the harbor?" Ocher asks.

"Certainly, I can use semaphore flags. Why?" Turner answers, turning back to look at Ocher.

"I'll explain later. Just signal them to remain offshore, but not too far," Ocher tells Turner.

Turner cuts two pieces of canvas from the sun screen and attaches them to a couple of pieces of straight driftwood. Turner, Ocher and Vincent walk to the end of what used to be a pier. Turner faces the incoming ship and with very precise movements presents the flags in various positions. Vincent and Ocher watch the ship.

"They're responding," Turner says. "The captain's coming about. There on the stern deck. The quartermaster's signaling back."

"What's he saying?" Ocher asks.

"Will comply," Vincent answers. "I know that captain. He's the best, but he'll want more. See, here comes the questions."

Over the next half hour, the ship sails in a circle as they exchange messages.

Vincent turns to Ocher, "My, my aren't you a devious bloke. The crew will like that."

The three men return to the camp. Ocher finds Stacey, "Your Mom and Dad are on the ship and they're fine. They know that you're here and safe."

"When can I see them?" Stacey asks, her voice cracking with emotion.

"Soon. Vincent, call in everybody. Everyone needs to know what's going to happen," Ocher says smiling.

"Yes, sir."

Chapter Thirty-Eight

After three days of planning, Ocher and the crew are comfortable with the ruse. Several canvas shelters have been constructed: a place for the men to eat, sleeping areas and a private area for Stacey.

English is near. Ocher can feel him watching. Several of the guards, with information from town, have reported English's movements.

Time to deliver the invitation.

A fight breaks out between the oncoming guards and the guards coming off duty. Both groups apparently have been drinking. The feud is loud, eventually leading to shoving and pushing. The melee moves away from the guarded perimeter, leaving the camp open.

Ocher's sitting by the fire, letting Turner and Vincent restore order.

"Hello, English," Ocher says, to the shadow just outside the camp fire glow.

"English?" comes the reply.

"Yes, English. That's what the lady you kidnapped calls you. That's the name you'll die with," Ocher responds in a calm voice.

"Little Orphan - or is it Ocher Jones now?" The shadow moves a little closer into the firelight.

"It doesn't matter, English. You're here, right where I wanted you."

The shadow doesn't respond immediately, realizing that perhaps he's overlooked something. "Those men, the guards. The fight was staged?"

"Yes. They didn't try to keep you out. They're to keep you in while we finish our business."

"You are prepared to die, Little Orphan?"

"The fear of death isn't a weapon you can use against me, English," Ocher says, refusing to use the assassin's title or name from the clan.

"The girl. I will take her life as well. The wench will pay for the poisoning..."

"That's my daughter you're talking about, mister. Where I come from that's a hanging offense," Lewis Livingston says, from the darkness behind Ocher.

"And she's a friend of mine," Ivan says, stepping forward so English can see him.

"Well done, Little Orphan. You have me surrounded. How many will die trying to keep me here?"

"Only one. You," Ocher replies, as Lewis and Ivan step into the light. Turner, Vincent and the other crewman ease from the darkness behind English.

"The only one missing is the girl. Tell her to come out from her tent. She should watch you die," English says, confidently.

"English, you're over-confident. She's on a ship at sea. She's been gone for days. We'll join her, soon."

Ocher watches English's eyes. The assassin's evaluating who's the greatest threat, other than Ocher. English will pick a target to divert Ocher's attention just long enough for an attack.

English has made his decision. He steps to his right just slightly, trying to draw Ocher in that direction. With a flick of his hand he directs a throwing star at Lewis, who's standing to Ocher's left. Ocher's ready and lunges in that direction. He reaches out and catches the deadly instrument in his left hand. His momentum carries him past Lewis.

The sound of a pistol shot pierces the night. As soon as Ocher clears Lewis's right hand, Lewis draws his Colt .44 and shoots English square in the chest.

"Damn," Ivan says. "I wanted to do that," holding out a butcher's knife. "I been sharpening this for days."

Ocher, pulling the throwing star out of his palm, walks over to English, "You're right about one thing, English. Little Orphan is dead. He died a long time ago. Jones. It's Ocher Jones."

"Little......" he whispers, "Orphan, they will not quit coming after you. There are only two of the tong left but they will not quit."

Ocher doesn't answer. There's no need. English can't hear him.

Ivan walks over to Ocher, "Let me see that hand. What's that thing?"

"It's a throwing star. Designed kind of like a throwing knife but with several blades, it's easily hidden and very dangerous. Sometimes dipped in poison."

"Is this one poisoned?" Lewis asks, watching Ivan pour whiskey on the wound.

"No. English never uses poison. He felt his skill was enough," Ocher answers, wincing at the whiskey now being poured onto his palm.

Ivan finishes wrapping Ocher's hand in a clean handkerchief, "Best I can do. Terrible waste of whiskey."

Ocher turns to face Turner and the rest of the men. "Gentlemen, you were great. I can't thank you enough for your protection and loyalty to our plot. I've been informed that the three ships we're waiting for have arrived. The day after tomorrow, if you'd be so kind, please join me for a banquet. There'll be plenty of liquor and some food."

"What about that?" Vincent asks, pointing at the body of English.

"Would you mind taking him to one of the mass graves and leaving him there. No need for ceremony," Ocher answers.

"Aye, Mister Jones. It'll be my pleasure," Vincent replies, motioning several of the men to pick up the body and place it in a wagon.

Chapter Thirty-Nine

Just as dawn breaks, Ocher, Lewis, and Ivan, with Turner at the helm, come alongside the *Anna Belle*. Turner stays with the boat to hook up the winch line to bring the boat aboard. The other three men scramble up a Jacob's Ladder to the deck.

Ocher sees Stacey. She's dressed in a clean blue flowered print dress, her hair shining in the dawn with a yellow ribbon tied in a bow. She's smiling at Ocher. Years of training have given him only two options: attack or retreat. Neither seems appropriate. He decides, based on watching the interaction of others, to settle on a hug. He moves forward.

Stacey senses his intention, but, "This is a brand new dress, Mr. Ocher Jones and you stink." It's at that moment she sees Ocher's hand, "What happened? Are you all right? Dad, are you all right? Ivan, where's Turner? What about English?" She forgets about her new dress and embraces Ocher.

Ocher doesn't move. He takes in the fresh fragrance of lavender, clean hair and soap.

"English is gone. Everybody's fine. My hand's fine. You'll see the rest of the men day after tomorrow."

Out of the corner of his eye Ocher can see Amanda rush by, headed toward Lewis. "Please, Amanda, let go of me," Lewis says, trying to pretend that he doesn't enjoy the attention of his wife.

"By your leave, Mr. Jones. I've made arrangements to moor the ships along the pier," Captain Kacey says, doffing his cap to Ocher. "I've signaled the other ships to weigh anchor and make for the harbor. Ivan can show you to your quarters where you may freshen up."

"Yes, Mr. Jones. Please do us all a favor and freshen up," Turner says, as he passes Ocher and Stacey. "The number two gig is secure, Captain."

"Thank you, Turner. Boatswain, weigh anchor and set the foresail."

The residents of Corpus have been busy. The rotting stores have been carted away. The salvageable lumber's stacked along the pier. The port's operating with ships coming and going. The Stanley Shipping fleet is moored stem to stern along the outermost pier by the time Ocher appears on deck.

"Don't you look just dandy," Turner says. "She's over there." He points toward the bow.

Stacey turns as Ocher approaches, "Dry land. I've had enough of the sea. Nice place to experience, but..."

"I agree. Soon you can head back home," Ocher says.

"Don't you mean we can head back home?" Stacey replies, with a question in her voice.

"You sure about the we part?" Ocher turns to look into Stacey's eyes.

"I'm sure."

"You know about..." Ocher starts.

"I know what I need to know. The rest is history."

"Ok." Ocher reaches out and takes Stacey's hand. "Then we can head home soon. But we have a lot of people to thank. So tomorrow..."

"Tomorrow will be exciting. A revelry. I learned that in finishing school. It'll be exciting to see all the people who helped us. And to say thank you," Stacey says, moving closer to Ocher.

"A party will be great. I'm going over to Stanley Shipping to meet with Jorge. There're a couple of surprises I want to arrange," Ocher says, removing his hand.

"Well, Mr. Jones, you go talk your business. Mother and I have a party to plan," Stacey kisses Ocher on the cheek and sashays away.

"If you break that girl's heart," Lewis says, walking up to Ocher smiling.

"I've seen what you can do with that Colt, Mr. Livingston. No need to worry," Ocher says to Lewis.

"What a glorious day," Ocher says as he turns the spit for the hind quarter of beef being carefully watched by Ivan.

The pier where the three ships *Anne Belle*, *Oleander* and the *Lantana* are moored is festooned with banners and pennants. The *S/V Argentine's* anchored off shore with a hired skeleton crew guarding the original crew. There're tables made with planks, roasting fires with beef, pork, shrimp and crabs being cooked. Beans, corn, and breads are baking aboard ship. And a couple of wagon loads of various liquid products are standing in the shade.

Ocher's surprised at the amount of provisions that Jorge Von Derr has managed to round up. He's sure that the coaxing of Amanda and Stacey has been an incentive. The men, who have had one day to prepare for the event, are bathed, shaved, dressed in their finest and for the moment sober. *They've earned this*, Ocher muses.

Ivan, under the supervision of Amanda and Stacey, declares, "We're ready." The crews assemble around the moored side of the *Anne Belle* as Jorge steps to the rail. "Before we begin, I have a couple of announcements to make." The men are eager to begin the feast and a couple of grumblings are heard.

"I'll keep this short," Jorge says. The cheers are overwhelming.

"Thank you all. As the local representative of Stanley Shipping I can't thank you enough for what you did to help in the rescue of Miss Stacey Livingston. I'm sure she and her family will be around to thank you personally."

Stacey, Amanda and Lewis are standing to the left of Jorge and wave to the men. They cheer and wave back.

"One last announcement. But I'm going to let Ocher make that," Jorge waves Ocher to join him aboard the ship.

"We don't want the food to get cold and the stuff in the shade to get warm," Ocher starts, "So. The *S/V Argentine* has been purchased by Stanley Shipping. It needs a crew and a captain. As a part owner I've recommended and it's been approved, that Boatswains Mate Caufield Turner will be promoted to Captain. He'll choose his own crew. All but one."

Turner, standing with the men on the pier, is promptly engulfed in men slapping his back and shaking his hand.

"Seaman Ulysses Vincent will be offered the position of ship's bosun," Ocher continues.

The men on the pier turn to look at Vincent, "I accept," he yells and turns to Captain Turner and salutes.

"Gentlemen. Enjoy," Ocher says, as he steps away from the rail.

Stacey's the focus of everyone's attention. The sailors, usually a raucous group, mind their manners. They abstain from typical sailor language and make extraordinary efforts in the proper use of eating with their hands and a spoon. She takes the time to speak to each and every one of the men who choose to come up to her. Some are too shy or intimidated by a beautiful, strong woman. Ocher gives up trying to stay by her side.

Ocher's not overlooked by the men, but Stacey's the focus.

"Captain Turner, a moment if you please," Ocher says, as the crowd thins around Turner. "Your first assignment will be an unpleasant one I'm afraid."

"Mr. Jones, Ocher, I suspect I know what must be done. My crew and I will return to the island and bury those men."

"Thank you, Captain."

"And it'll be my pleasure to set the previous crew of the *Argentine* ashore somewhere appropriate."

"Again, thank you."

"Ocher, I speak for my crew and I suspect all of the men here. You or Miss Stacey ever need us, for anything, say the word. Don't know how we'll fare ashore but these are good men and we'll answer the call."

Ocher smiles at Turner and starts to respond.

"Thank you, Captain," Stacey says, as she walks alongside Ocher and takes his hand.

"By your leave, Miss Stacey, Mr. Jones," Turner says, with a break in his voice, as he tips his cap, turns and walks away.

"They're not much different from cowboys, good cowboys, that is," Lewis says, as he approaches Stacey and Ocher, Amanda on his arm.

"I don't understand," Ocher says, turning toward Lewis.

"They ride for the brand. A good cowhand, and apparently a good sailor, has an allegiance to his employer. From what I've observed, these men ride for the brand," Lewis explains.

Ocher's silent for a few minutes. He looks at the crowd of men gathering in small groups, disbanding and moving to form other groups. "Allegiance. I thought I understood the word, but until now not the real meaning."

"You had an allegiance to your, what did you call it, a tong? But in name only. Your allegiance is to, well, what you think is the right thing to do," Amanda offers. "We've seen that in you from the beginning. Now you're beginning to understand it as well."

A dark shadow engulfs the group as Jorge Von Derr approaches the gathering. His seven foot frame blocks the sun. "I have a telegram concerning the ranch and a letter from Mom. I think this celebration's going to continue for a while. The men have gravitated toward the wagon with the potables."

"Potables?" Lewis asks.

"Liquor, Dad," Stacey answers.

"Oh. Well they certainly earned a good time," Lewis says, smiling at Stacey.

"The shipping office didn't suffer any damage. Let's go there and discuss the news," Jorge offers.

Jorge pours coffee for Lewis, Amanda, Stacey and Ocher. After pouring himself a cup, he sits down behind his desk. He holds up a sheaf of papers, "Mom's letter. I won't read the whole thing," he sets the letter down. "As you know, Mom and Dad took the whole family to the Double LL to help out. Jeremy's there as well. We'll get to that in a minute. Not that your ranch hands needed it, but ..."

Lewis chuckles, "From what Ocher's told us your whole family is tall. I bet the townsfolk were surprised by that."

"The good news is that the ranch is still standing, actually both ranches. The older boys are at your ranch, Ocher, with Bug. From what I can gather Bug has his hands full. The younger boys are, and I use this word with caution, helping with the ranch chores. The whole gang gathers for supper so Mom can inspect the boys and make sure they're washing at least once a day."

"How many boys are there?" Stacey asks.

"Only eight. There are three in college."

"Eight is plenty," Ocher adds.

"I've been reading men and sign for a long time, Jorge. What's the rest of it?" Lewis asks, as he leans forward.

Jorge pushes the letter aside and picks up a telegram. "Ocher, your instincts about the La Beaux crew were correct. You did miss one detail, but I'll get to that in a minute."

"See, you aren't perfect, Mr. Jones," Stacey teases and reaches over for Ocher's hand.

Ocher just shakes his head.

"When La Beaux and company arrived at the ranch they had a death certificate and a will. They also had a buyer for both ranches. Well, when the documents were presented to the traveling judge, your friend Holt, several Pinkerton agents and my brother Jeremy, the lawyer, were present."

"I can't wait to face Miss La Beaux and give her a piece of my mind," Stacey says, squeezing the blood out of Ocher's hand.

"Miss Stacey, you won't get that opportunity on two counts," Jorge says.

"I don't understand," Stacey remarks.

"Based on the evidence brought west by the Pinkerton's and La Beaux's efforts to steal the ranch, Jeremy got a quick conviction and the judge sentenced the whole bunch to be hanged. They were."

"That's seems a bit harsh," Ocher says.

"Maybe, but consider this. Miss La Beaux is, was, Mr. George La Beaux and was wanted for murder in several states. The rest of them were co-conspirators to the murders. They were taken to Austin and hanged."

"That makes sense," Ocher comments.

"Yes it does," Amanda adds.

"What does?" Lewis asks.

"When I was in Japan," Ocher starts, "I watched Kabuki Dancers. A play put on by performers. The women were actually men. I thought something was off with La Beaux. It would have been tough to prove. I just let it go."

"I suspected the same thing," Amanda continues with the conversation. "When we first met, she or he offered to shake Ocher's hand. Women don't do that."

"I reckon I was too mad to notice any of that. I just wanted to strangle the women or man," Lewis says, shaking his head.

"I can't believe that Maggie and Franklin were involved in that. I just can't believe it," Stacey says, sitting back in her chair.

"Well, Miss Stacey, you are correct. Your friends left here ahead of the rest of the troupe and went to Pine Springs. They found Holt and testified against the rest of them. I don't know where they went. They were given immunity. The rest were predators, Miss Stacey. They got caught," Jorge says, holding up the letter from his folks.

There are no responses from anyone.

"Now, I have rounded up two wagons, horses and supplies for your journey home. You can leave as soon as you want."

"I'd like to say my farewells to the crews, in the morning before we leave," Ocher says.

"The ships are being provisioned this afternoon and are scheduled to leave on the tide tomorrow. I'm sure the crews would like to see you all before they sail. Believe me, this is a story that'll be told for a long time. You, Miss Stacey, are the pride of the fleet," Jorge says, smiling broadly at Stacey.

"Cowboys and sailors," says Stacey. "I'm proud to know them all. I'll miss the men but not the sea. I'd rather have hot desert sand between my toes than that other stuff."

Chapter Forty

Lewis, now back in his element, dry land, starts to bellow, "Everybody up. We're burning daylight."

"They're as anxious as you to start home. Everybody's already up, dear," Amanda says, walking past Lewis.

The Stanley Shipping building, a two-story brick structure, was built with accommodations on the upper level. Lewis and Amanda are in one room, Stacey in a private room. Ocher takes the first room at the top of the stairs.

"Good morning, Amanda, Lewis," Ocher says, as the Livingstons reach the bottom of the stairs. "Coffee?"

"Yes, please," Lewis says.

"The wagons are out front, horses hitched up, provisions checked, we're ready. Stacey just went out to stow her gear," Ocher says, pouring two cups of coffee.

Amanda gives Ocher a mischievous look, "Stowing her gear? Heavens you've been around those sailors too long. Cowboys don't stow anything."

Lewis starts to say something, but Stacey enters the room, her hair freshly washed, her tanned complexion glowing, her smile filling the room. "Good morning. Dad, I have arranged the provisions so you can stow, I mean put, your gear and Mom's kit just behind the wagon's seat."

"Thank you, sweetheart. I guess the only thing to do now is say our goodbyes and head home," Amanda beams at her daughter.

Lewis looks at Ocher, nods toward the door and proceeds outside to the wagons.

The wagons approach the wharf, Lewis and Amanda in the lead, Stacey and Ocher following. The three ships are abuzz with activity. There're men aloft checking sails, lines and rigging. Men on deck are doing the same. Suddenly a boatswain's whistle trills and all activity stops. The men aloft start down and the men on deck move toward the dock. By the time the wagons pull abeam of the ships, all hands, seamen, and officers are on the pier.

Captain Turner, at the front of the assembly says, "Miss Stacey, would you be so kind as to step down. The men have something for you."

Ocher gets off the wagon and takes Stacey's hand as she steps down.

"I don't know," he says, answering Stacey's puzzled look.

Stacey walks toward Captain Turner and stops just short of him. Ocher stands back a few paces.

"As you know, Miss Stacey, I ain't much of a talker but the men wanted me to..., well they have a gift for you. They don't want you to forget them. They, me, well we, never met such a fine young woman. Pretty, smart and tough as nails. Well..."

Vincent steps up beside Turner and hands him a long, off-white, elephant tusk.

Stacey can see black carvings on the tusk.

"We all pitched in and bought this here tusk. Some of the crew have a gift for carving. Sailors call it scrimshaw. The scrimshaw shows the three ships. See this small boat here?" Turner points to one of the carved scenes, "That's us in the ketch. Here we are in the storm," he points again. "On the back are the names of the crew, so's you won't forget."

Ocher steps forward to take the five foot, heavy tusk from Turner.

"I don't know what to say," Stacey says, through her tears. "I'll never forget any of you. Thank you. This must have taken..."

"Miss Stacey, I been a sailor all my life. We sailors don't generally pass up free liquor, but most of what was in that wagon's still there. The men worked all night instead of drinking. I wouldn't have believed it, but it's true," Captain Turner says.

Stacey looks at Turner, "Captain, if you could tell your men to, stand down, or whatever the phrase is, I intend to hug every one of them."

Turner smiles a big smile at the ship's company. "At ease."

Stacey wades into the surrounding sea of sailors hugging and thanking each and every one. Some more than once.

The boatswain's pipe shrills. "Stand by to get underway," Vincent hails.

Stacey, Ocher and the Livingstons emerge from the crowd of sailors and make their way toward the wagons. The crowd of assembled men breaks apart and reassemble on the appropriate ship. By the time the tusk is properly packed, the lead ship, *S/V Anne Belle,* is making sail and departing.

Jorge Von Derr ambles his seven foot frame over to the lead wagon, "Amanda, Lewis, I wish we'd met under different circumstances. But, what an adventure. It's been a pleasure." He reaches out and kisses Amanda's hand and shakes Lewis's. He walks slowly to the other wagon.

"Jorge. I'm through crying, but thank you again," Stacey says, holding out both hands toward Jorge.

"I ain't too big to cry, Stacey. You are two of my most favorite people. Well, you are, of course, my favorite. He," Jorge points toward Ocher, "him I can tolerate."

"Thanks, Jorge, for everything," Ocher says.

"Give Mom and Dad a hug when you get back to the ranch, will you?" Jorge says, and walks away quickly.

As Lewis starts the wagon toward the road west, the last of the ships clears the harbor.

Ocher and Stacey stay quiet as they ride through the town of Corpus Christi. The rebuilding is well underway. In almost every block there are work parties doing construction, cleaning or burning debris. The further west the wagons travel, the less damage is seen. At noon they stop to rest the horses.

"Ain't been seasick all morning," Lewis grins over a cup of coffee. "Reckon my seat end ain't used to that wagon, yet."

"It doesn't seem real. Heading home and all that's happened, does it?" Stacey says, to no one in particular.

"I reckon there's all kinds of fancy words can be said about what's happened but they don't mean much. What's done is done," Lewis says.

"I'm looking forward to meeting Ollie, Marta and those boys," Amanda adds.

"Saddle up. Let's get moving," Lewis barks, throwing his coffee dregs on the fire.

The day goes by with Ocher and Stacey engaged in small talk. Ocher wants to get back to the ranches and meet up with Holt. Ocher wants to know what's the proper thing to do about

Stacey is. Holt will have the answers. If not, Ollie will certainly know. At least he hopes so.

On the third night as Ocher and Stacey are fishing for supper, he asks, "Want to talk about it?"

"No. I'm going to think about all the good men that helped me, us. Those others I don't want to remember. Thinking about them keeps them alive. They're gone and I want them to stay gone," Stacey answers.

Ocher understands perfectly. But he can't forget English's last words, "There're two more left." He knows who they are and will remember them until it's time to forget.

The remaining days and nights go by comfortably and quietly. The conversation reminds Ocher of high tide and low tide. The further they get from the sea, the less talk about it. The closer they get to the ranch, the more they anticipate the arrival.

It's just a notion but Ocher feels like there's someone following them. It's not worth bothering the rest of the caravan. He'll stay vigilant though.

The one thing they don't anticipate is notoriety. After about five days on the trail, the caravan stops by a small prairie settlement to replenish their supplies. The hangings and the reason for them is the topic of conversation virtually everywhere.

"You must be those folks the Rangers helped out," the store clerk observes. "Hey Mavis," he yells toward the back of the store. "You'll never guess who's out here."

Mavis, the town gossip, does her job. By the time the travelers gather their provisions and walk back to the wagons, the whole town's standing around.

There're no more stops, by both wagons, at least, when provisions are needed. Ocher or Lewis ride in alone while the wagons stay in hiding.

One day just at the nooning, Ocher walks away from the fire and stands just outside the gathering.

"What is it, Ocher?" Lewis asks, walking up beside Ocher. "I been around you long enough to see something's been bothering you."

"There's someone out there following us. Thing is I get the feeling there's more than one."

Lewis stands silently looking out toward the rolling hills, "Amanda and Stacey both can shoot if needed."

"I know. You ain't bad yourself. Best post a night guard starting tonight."

"Yep."

Over supper the night watch is assigned. There's no argument.

The following day the terrain changes from barren rolling hills to scrub brush with islands of trees and the occasional arroyo.

About an hour before sunset, Lewis shoots a deer. They settle into one of the tree islands with an elevated dry wash behind them. The camp site's selected for defense. At least that's the thought.

"We're protected on three sides. We should see anybody coming from that open side, unless." Ocher says to Lewis looking east at their back trail. "I got a feeling it's gonna to get crowded around here and soon."

It's just a small thing. A light breeze is coming from the west but the branch on the bush on the dry wash moves in the opposite direction. Ocher reaches down to pick up his plate for supper and uses the move to disguise his interest in the bush. Before he can focus on the dry wash, four men, riding hard, head into the open end of the camp. Two men ride directly in and the other two approach at wide angles from the left and right.

"Amanda, Stacey, get over behind that wagon," Lewis says, in a calm voice, pointing toward the wagon positioned for just this purpose. He draws his Colt and checks the loads.

Ocher doesn't want the riders to have any advantage by getting inside the camp. He steps away from the camp directly at the two men riding straight in. The men don't slow. The riders are approximately four feet apart and headed straight at Ocher.

Ocher scrapes his plate off with his left hand and turns to the same side. The rider on the right is slightly behind the rider on the left. Ocher sails the plate straight at the left man on horseback. The blue porcelain plate strikes the oncoming horseman right below the chin in the Adam's apple. He reaches up with both hands to his neck, losing the reins and topples off the horse, hitting the ground in a explosion of dust.

Ocher waits for the man on the right as the rider gallops straight at him shooting at the same time. Ocher ignores the gun fire and times his jump just as the man reaches him. Ocher reaches over and takes the man's chin in his right hand as he places his left behind his head. Momentum does the rest. When Ocher's feet hit the ground, the man's head is facing backward while the rest of his body is facing forward. The rider tumbles to the ground.

Lewis yells, "Look out."

Ocher turns toward the first man. The man is getting off the ground and reaching for his gun. Ocher knows that he can't cover the distance between himself and the man reaching for his gun. He can see a paper tag from a tobacco pouch hanging out of the man's left shirt pocket. With the speed of a rattlesnake, Ocher reaches back, taking his throwing knife from the sheaf between his shoulder blades and throws. The knife hits the paper tag, pinning it to the man's chest. The hasp of the knife stops just as it touches the man's shirt. The rest of the knife is buried in his heart.

The person on the dry wash enters the confrontation. The sound of a shot is unmistakable, a buffalo gun. The impact of the bullet is also unmistakable.

Ocher sees the outrider on his right leave his saddle as the .50 caliber slug hits him in the chest. The man lands in the dirt ten feet behind his horse.

Holt. Ocher thinks.

The other outrider's seen enough. He turns his horse and gallops away as a second shot from the buffalo gun resounds. It misses.

Lewis turns toward the dry wash at the sound of the first shot, aiming his .44 at the shooter. Lewis takes a quick glance to see what the shooter is firing at. He sees the outrider go down. Still, he keeps his aim on the dry wash. Even after the second shot, Lewis does not let down his guard.

"In the camp," comes the hail from the dry wash. "I'm friendly. I'm coming in." Holt stands up from behind a mesquite bush and walks down the shifting sand of the hill.

Amanda and Stacey emerge from under the safety of the wagon. Before they can speak there're several pistol shots well away from the camp coming from the direction the escaping out rider has taken.

Ocher walks to the small gathering by the wagon, "I was hoping that was you back there."

"How in the world could you have known?" Holt demands.

"Saw the bush move against the wind," Ocher replies.

Lewis is looking off in the distance, "More company. A man leading a horse." As the rider gets closer, "That's the horse that other fellow was riding. He with you, Holt?"

"Nope."

Stacey remains very quiet, avoiding eye contact with Ocher.

Ocher watches the man approach. "That fellow's a good friend of mine. Kemen Cortez."

Holt glares at Ocher, "A friend? Baja Cortez is a friend of yours?"

"As good a friend as you are Holt. Today he's Kemen and only that," Ocher glares back.

The Ranger's torn between his friend and his duty. Finally, "Kemen it is. "

"Hola, in the camp," Baja hails.

"Come on in, and welcome," Ocher replies.

"Amigo, it is good to see you again," Baja says, with a smile, looking at Holt and the Ranger's Badge pinned to his vest.

Baja's smile gets even bigger as he sees Stacey, "Amigo, this must be the senorita with the lavender scarf. It is a great pleasure to meet you, senorita." Baja tips his sombrero.

"Nice horse, Baja – I mean Kemen," Holt says, with a challenge in his voice.

"Si, Senor Ranger. A little bird told me that a man with no guns was crossing Texas carrying valuable jewels. The jewels were to be used as ransom for a *hermosa*, 'beautiful,' senorita."

"I heard the same rumor," Holt states.

"Who else could it be but mi amigo. The same little bird told me that there were some bad hombres following this man to steal the jewels. And take the senorita. So we followed those men," Baja points toward the men on the ground, "To discourage them."

"The horse?" Holt asks again.

"He did not wish to discuss the matter and drew his pistol. I now have a new horse," Baja answers. "I see that there are three newly acquired horses here. They belong to you, Senor Ranger?"

Holt just shakes his head, "Step down and help me bury these men," Holt orders.

"Senora, senorita, the food smells delicious. I have eaten his cooking." He nods toward Ocher. "Digging in this dirt will sharpen my appetite. Could a poor vaquero beg a little supper and some coffee?"

Amanda just smiles, "Of course, Mr. Cortez, and you'll spend the night here with us. Isn't that right Holt?"

Holt's expression doesn't change, "I've had worse friends. But I do want to hear the story of you two." Holt looks at Baja and then Ocher.

Stacey says nothing. Her expression remains neutral. She avoids making eye contact with Ocher.

Ocher's amazed at the story Baja tells about the adventure to St. Louis. Ocher knows he'd been a participant but barely recognizes the events as told by Baja. After much laughter, with the fire burned down to ashes, the group breaks apart and beds down.

Stacey has remained quiet during the evening and continues to avoid eye contact with Ocher.

"Baja, tell your men thank you for guarding the camp when you see them," Ocher whispers to Baja as they stake out their piece of ground for the night.

"How do you... never mind. I remember, I said we. I will tell them, amigo." Baja shakes his head in amazement.

The next morning Baja's shaving down by the creek. A small polished steel plate hanging from a tree limb acts as a mirror.

Holt walks up, "I see your holster hanging there. I should arrest you, Baja."

"Si, Senor Holt. But mi amigo with the rifle out there would probably shoot you."

"That's what I figured. Ocher told me you had associates guarding the camp."

"You shoot me, that fellow out there shoots you. Ocher loses two good friends. Not so good."

"I'd much rather have Ocher as a friend than you in prison. Too high a price to pay."

"Si. Killing you would cost too much. You and I are like two bulls in a pasture. That one, however, is the king bull, amigo," Baja smiles.

"Reckon you're right about that. You stay on your side of the pasture and I'll stay on mine, Baja."

"Si, Senor Ranger, Holt."

Chapter Forty-One

The sun's rises, dissolving the dark of the night.

"Morning, sweetheart," Amanda says, as she sits down next to Stacey. "Long night?"

"Yes," Stacey continues to look into the fire. "I want to ride with you for a while?"

"Ok. Want to talk about it?" Amanda says, putting her arm around her daughter.

"No, not now. I don't know, Mom. I need to think."

"Ok. I'll tell your dad."

Lewis approaches the two women, "Something wrong?"

Amanda looks up and nods toward Ocher.

"Had to happen sooner or later. Hearing about it ain't the same as seeing what Ocher's capable of."

"Dad, I want to ride with Mom for a while."

"Sure, honey, sure."

The morning's normal camp talk's forgotten. The chores are completed without any comments or banter. Amanda and Stacey take the lead with Lewis and Ocher following. Holt and Baja take the outrider positions. Even the horses sense the tension and wait to be cajoled into action.

Abruptly Ocher states, "The ranch is yours. As soon as we get back, I'll sign the deed over to you and leave. I'd appreciate it if you'd keep Bug on. He's a good man."

"Whoa, cowboy," Lewis responds. "Running away don't suit you."

"I'm not running. Just, well... Lewis, I brought this down on you all. She deserves better."

Lewis twitches the reins, "That ain't your decision to make. That's hers. Not to put too fine a point on it, but, as that fella English said, 'There's two more out there.' They came for her once. What's to stop them a second time?"

"Me. I'll hunt them and do what I was trained to do."

"Mom. He killed those two men with just his hands," Stacey blurts out after squirming in the wagon seat and brooding for several hours.

"Yes, he did," Amanda says calmly.

"I don't know. He scared me."

"How?"

"How what? I don't understand."

Amanda stays quiet while working the team up a slight incline. "Child, how many men has your dad shot or shot at with evil intent? You think that we just decided to homestead the ranch and it was without conflict? How about those men you poisoned?"

"That's different, Mom.."

"Is it? How?"

"I don't know, just different."

"How long have you known that young man?"

"A little over a year."

"In that year can you name one thing that Ocher's done for his own benefit?"

Stacey starts and stops several responses, "No, I can't."

"Is he dangerous? I'll answer that. Yes, he is. Probably the most dangerous man I've ever met. The question then, 'Is he dangerous to you?'"

"Mom, I don't know."

The days continue, the terrain changes from dusty, to dry and dusty and finally to sandy and barren.

It's been too hot to even have any conversation, but just after stopping to water the horses and grab a drink themselves, Lewis turns to Ocher, "Ocher, you left that life behind once, now you want to go back to that?"

"No, but I have no choice."

"Oh, I think you have a lot of choices. You're just taking the easiest one. A martyr we don't need."

"I don't think that's fair..."

"Maybe, but you going on the prowl for those other two assassins leaves us to fend for ourselves. Is that fair? Making choices that affect Stacey, Amanda, your ranch, my ranch, and lots of others. Just taking it all on yourself. Is that fair?"

"No, but what if..."

"The safety of my family is not a 'what if,' Ocher. From what you've told us your whole life's been just you. It ain't that way anymore. It ain't just you and you alone, young man. Stacey may or may not ... well, she may or may not. That's her choice. And as you said, you brought this to our door step. One last thing. A while back you stopped me from a bull-headed decision to confront Boyd on his terms. That was good advice then and it's good advice now."

Ocher watches the dust rise from the lead wagon for a long time, "Lewis, I didn't know my dad, but I get the feeling that he would have said the same thing you did. I'll stay and run the ranch, and, as you say, read the sign."

"Have faith, son. Have faith."

For the remainder of the trip Ocher busies himself with camp chores, night watches that don't need night watches, and giving Stacey space. Lewis spends the days discussing the ranch plans with Ocher and watching Ocher and Stacey avoid making decisions.

Holt and Baja navigate the camp and do the same dance of avoidance as Ocher and Stacey are doing but for different reasons.

As the two wagons approach Spring Hill, Texas, Amanda leads the team around the town and heads directly toward the Double LL. Just at supper time, the wagons arrive.

It's like ants cascading from an ant hill: Ollie, Marta, the kids, the ranch hands and Bug converge on the wagons. Ollie scoops up Ocher as Marta does the same with Stacey. Ollie, after almost squeezing the life out Ocher, sets him down. The kids mob Ocher, then run over to Stacey, finally back on the ground, then back to Ocher. Total pandemonium.

Marta assumes command. "Supper's on the table, if anyone's interested." No one seems interested.

The whole scene finally takes one step back from pandemonium, into frenzy and then settles into confusion.

The ranch hands take care of offloading the gear from the Livingston's wagon. The raucous scene is too much for Bug and he whispers to Ocher, "I'll grab a bite then take your wagon up to the ranch. You and the boys can come up when you've a mind to."

Ocher nods, "Good to see you, Bug."

Marta tries again, "Supper's getting cold."

Ollie makes an announcement that surprises no one, "Please, I'm hungry."

The eight kids remain, surrounding Ocher, each talking over the other one about the adventure they've been sharing. This small knot is at the end of the chow line. Ocher moves the group into the kitchen, gets a plate, returns outside and is immediately surrounded again by the boys.

Just after sundown Ollie and Lewis, after conferring with the women, announce, "Ocher, you Holt, Baja and the older boys go on up to the High Range for the night. Marta and I will be along in the morning. This is Amanda's kitchen and that's that. On Sunday we'll meet here for dinner and make our plans. I expect all of you," Ollie looks at Baja and Holt, "to be here."

"Morning, Vernon isn't it?"

"Yes, Miss Stacey."

Stacey sits down in the chair next to Vernon, rocking in a chair. "You're the youngest? How old are you, Vernon?"

"Near as we can tell, eleven. That's what PaPa Ollie says." Vernon rocks back and forth a couple of times. "Miss Stacey, you like Uncle Ocher, don't you?"

Stacey doesn't answer. She takes a sip of coffee. Finally she manages, "I do, but ..."

"He's scary. Not scary afraid scary but scary. None of us boys are afraid of him, but we know how scared he can make other people. Kinda like PaPa Ollie."

"I'm not sure what you mean, Vernon."

Vernon rocks back and forth again, "PaPa Ollie's a giant. He can scare you, if he's a mind to, by just looking at you. Uncle Ocher's different. When he lived with us, all of us boys would try and sneak up on him or catch him off guard. Never could. And we heard stories about how he scared away bad people. But we ain't, 'scuse me, aren't, afraid of him. We call him uncle but he's more a big brother. We know nothing will happen to any of us with him or PaPa Ollie around."

"It sounds like you're going to miss him when you all go back to San Francisco," Stacey says, turning in the chair to look at Vernon.

"Yes, Miss Stacey, we all will. That's why we came here. To help part of the family, like he'd do for any of us."

Stacey is quiet long enough for her coffee to turn cold. She stands and dumps the contents of the cup into one of the hanging gourds.

"I heard you talking to your mom. Would you miss him if he left?"

Stacey doesn't answer Vernon. She just walks back into the house.

Sunday noon arrives. Long barn siding boards have been placed on saw horses. Bed sheets have been laid over the top as tablecloths. There isn't an inch that isn't covered by plates, silverware and food.

The table is set to accommodate Ollie and Marta with eight boys, Ocher and Bug. Lewis,

Amanda, Stacey and three ranch hands, with Holt and Baja making an even twenty.

Ocher's standing with Ollie, Holt and Baja watching the comings and goings of the boys when Vernon approaches.

"Miss Stacey asked me to give you this," Vernon says, and hands a bandana to Ocher. He can smell the lavender.

Baja looks up as Stacey and her father walk out the kitchen door, "Amigo, I think she's made a decision." He points with his chin toward Stacey.

Stacey has her father's arm as they step off the porch. She has a yellow ribbon in her hair.

Ocher ties the bandana around his neck.

Coming soon –

Ocher's Fire
Ocher Jones Western Series –
Book Four

Synopsis of Ocher's Fire –

A fire. A robbery. Ocher's pursuit of the robbers leads him into a very hostile environment, the cold.

A warning from the past haunts Ocher during his chase. *"There are two assassins left. They will find you."*

Contact Information:

Mike Gipson

msguscg@gmail.com

www.ingramcontent.com/pod-product-compliance
Lightning Source LLC
Chambersburg PA
CBHW031727170626
46808CB00005B/1919